ECHO DE PARIS

JOURNAL LITTÉRAIRE ET POLITIQUE DU MATIN

RÉDACTION ET ADMINISTRATION : 16, RUE DU CROISSANT

VALENTIN SIMOND

Publiés de première et deuxième page exclusivement des bureaux à « ECHO DE PARIS », 16, rue du Croissant

LE CHERCHEUR D'OR

LES MINUTES DE LA VIE

OCTAVE MIRBEAU

NOUVELLES À LA MAIN

A MARSEI...

IN THE SKY

OCTAVE MIRBEAU

TRANSLATED BY ANN STERZINGER

With Claire Nettleton and Robert Ziegler

NINE-BANDED BOOKS

In the Sky by Octave Mirbeau

Translation copyright © 2015 Ann Sterzinger, Nine-Banded Books

Preface © 2015 Claire Nettleton

Dans le ciel (*In the Sky*) was first published in serial form in *L'Echo de Paris* between September 1892 and May 1893. The present text was translated from the French by Ann Sterzinger with assistance by Claire Nettleton and Robert Ziegler.

Special thanks to Anita Dalton and Pierre Michel.

ISBN 10: 0990733513
ISBN 13: 978-0-9907335-1-5

Published by

    Nine-Banded Books
    Post Office Box 1862
    Charleston, WV 25327
    United States of America

    NineBandedBooks.com

First printing, June 2015

Cover art: "Avenue of Poplars at Sunset," 1884, by Vincent van Gogh, manipulated

Cover design by Kevin I. Slaughter

Contents

INTRODUCTION

*His art disturbed me with its audacity and violence.
It moved me, terrified me, almost, like the visions of
a madman. And I think there was indeed madness
infused throughout his works.*

—Octave Mirbeau, *In the Sky*

Under swirling stars in the fiery moonlight, beneath
twisted branches, stands a madman with an easel. The
violent streaks on his canvas follow no rules and have
no precedent. Images appear like seeds bursting into
majestic sunflowers, only to shrivel, die, and disappear beneath the overwhelming, soul-crushing sky.

Such is the resonant image of the fictional Lucien,
surrogate for Vincent van Gogh and so many mar-
ginalized and frustrated geniuses who were misun-
derstood in their own time. Octave Mirbeau (1848–
1917) first published *In the Sky* in installments in
L'Echo de Paris between September 1892 and May
1893. Pierre Michel and Jean-Francois Nivet, promi-
nent Mirbeau scholars, edited and published the work

as an unfinished novella in 1989.[1] Over a century after its original publication, *In the Sky* now appears in English for the first time.

In the Sky is a tale of a meek and self-doubting writer's friendship with a Faustian painter who descends into madness. It reveals the symbiotic relationship between writing and painting as well as the close proximity between genius and insanity. Though he is better known as a novelist, playwright, and anarchist, Mirbeau was also an art critic and an avid defender of avant-gardists such as Van Gogh, Paul Gauguin, Camille Claudel, and Pierre Bonnard. He also greatly admired the work of Claude Monet, Auguste Rodin, and Camille Pissaro, with whom he corresponded.[2] Mirbeau's ties to these visual artists and his fervent combat against stifling ideologies and social injustice make his works still relevant today. His novels and plays have been translated into thirty languages, and his best-known work, *Diary of a Chambermaid* (1900), a novel that unmasks bourgeois hypocrisy and denounces domestic servitude, has been adapted into several films.

Despite his popularity, Mirbeau himself could be described as an eccentric genius. He thrived at the margins of society. He was plagued by frustration and by the fear of being unable to create. Claude Monet, one of the most celebrated painters today, shared with Mirbeau that he suffered similar feelings of inadequacy, confid-

---

1   Michelle, Pierre and Jean François Nivet. *Dans le ciel*. By Octave Mirbeau. Caen: l'Echoppe, 1989.

2   Michelle & Nivet. *Op cit.* "Préface."

ing that he had burned many of his own paintings.[3] *In the Sky* reflects this inner struggle. Reminiscent of Monet and Van Gogh, Lucien's rejection of academic and social authority gives birth to visionary art that defies convention. His philosophy of art as an organic process that evolves and transforms echoes Darwinian and Lamarckian themes,[4] but Lucien's defiance also makes him unable to function in society.

The trope of the "mad artist" is common to nineteenth century literature for good reason. Mirbeau wrote during a time of political and social unrest and cultural instability. *Fin-de-siècle* France had endured multiple regime changes, had suffered a Prussian invasion and bloody uprisings, and had become increasingly industrialized and urbanized.[5] During this transformative time, the antiquated values of the *Académie des Beaux-Arts* no longer made sense. The Impressionists and Post-Impressionists captured the frenzy of modernity while their close attention to the tranquil beauty of nature also provided respite from it. But their revolt against stylistic convention and their lack of artistic patronage meant that such artists were often dismissed as bohemians, as brutes and mad degenerates. Pseudoscientific interpretations of evolutionary theory as well as neurological studies by Jean-Martin Charcot reinforced such beliefs.[6]

3   "Claude Monet au Musée Marmottan." Musée Marmottan. 6 April 2015. Web.

4   Nettleton, Claire. "L'Animal et l'esthétique nihiliste de *Dans le ciel.*" *Cahiers Octave Mirbeau* 20 (2013): 63–79.

5   Jensen, Robert. *Marketing Modernism in Fin-de-siècle Europe.* Princeton: Princeton, 1994.

6   Nordau, Max. *Degeneration.* New York: D. Appleton and Company, 1895.

In the Sky inherits the figure of the marginal artist found in Honoré Balzac's *The Unknown Masterpiece* (1831) and Émile Zola's *The Masterpiece* (1886). But Mirbeau, a shocking, scandalous, and decadent writer, takes the archetype further. The author of *The Torture Garden* (1899), a sadistic account of a hysteric who delights in observing torture, and "Dingo" (1913), a story of an insightful yet murderous dog, has left us with a singular portrait of the artist as assassin. Lucien annihilates the canvas and mutilates himself. Mirbeau's vivid, fragmented prose reflects the unraveling of rational thought—creating an aesthetic of brute violence, of decay and utter nihilism. Ironically, it is this void felt by the characters—the tremendous emptiness that weighs on their shoulders, the pressure to create, the terror that their art will never amount to their vision, the blank canvas as vast as the sky—that is the beginning of all creation. This paradox of creative impotence is part of what Robert Ziegler, a celebrated scholar of Decadent literature (who also advised the brilliant author Ann Sterzinger on this faithful translation), describes as Mirbeau's "Nothing Machine."[1] His iconoclastic writing destroys falsity, leaving only incomplete fragments in its wake.

As an imagined voyage into the psyche of some of the most renowned artists in history, *In the Sky* inspires us to rethink the creative process. Could our most beloved works of art be products of mental instability and emotional turmoil? What is the line

1   Ziegler, Robert. *The Nothing Machine: The Fiction of Octave Mirbeau*. Amsterdam: Rodopi, 2007.

of demarcation between creativity and psychosis? Could our own frustrations and anxieties actually be the seeds of creation, ready to germinate into flowers that spring forth like shooting stars in the night sky?

—*Claire Nettleton*
April, 2015

In the Sky

Chapter I

It had been a long time since I promised my friend X that I would go visit him in his solitude. But you know how it goes . . . my life was full of business affairs, and more tempting pleasures. Not to mention my bottomless cowardly laziness, my spineless and confused misgivings, all of which kept me, year after year, from fulfilling this promise, which I'd made without really meaning it anyway, just so as not to offend such an old beloved friend by refusing him straight out. Poor old X . . . ! Ah! The past is coming back to me . . . Our past . . . the memory brings up vivid emotion, but nothing too deep—isn't that strange and anti-literary? Poor X! What a good and upright nature! What faithfulness! What a delicately devoted soul! . . . Together we'd lived out our first hopes and joys in Paris, and we mingled our two burdens of poverty to create a common wealth. Our friendship was so touching! How far away from me it all is already! X could have made a name in literature for himself. He was incredibly gifted. But he was too sensitive. Life was killing him . . . In the struggle that sweeps everyone away, we have no time to help a dear friend. And in any case, what good would it have done?

X didn't know how to extricate himself from hardship. His naiveté discouraged me, really. Even as the rest of us rose little by little, he insisted on staying down . . . One day, he inherited a bit of land from an old relative in a distant region.

"I believe," he told me, "that I should go there . . . It seems that the solitude, the meditation . . . Wouldn't it? . . . What do you think? The great horizons . . . the vast sky!"

"Absolutely!" I said. "You're right; if I were you, I would get out of here."

"All right then. Off I go . . . "

"Good for you! That's just the thing. Goodnight."

He left . . . and that was fifteen years ago!

We quickly forget friends who are far away or unhappy. Despite his begging letters and my promises, I kept pushing back the date of the trip. Let's be frank: I cringed at the thought of his uncomfortable rooms, his sad meals, his stinking maidservant and above all—oh! Above all, the drawn-out tête-à-têtes with a being who had become alien to my way of life, whom I imagined as a dirty body in dirty clothes—his mind smothered in peasant slime, with a long beard, sordid hair, and ideas and moral habits that were more sordid still . . . .

I want to be generous, but only under the condition that it doesn't cost me anything, and that my generosity serves to redouble my own selfish pleasure and vain joy. So what pleasure do you suppose there was in this? And how was I going to brag to my pretty girlfriends about how I spent my country vacation with this poor devil?

But his last letter was so insistent, its sickly endearments betraying such an intense, painful desire to see me, that I resolved to undertake this nasty trip, reasoning to myself: "After all, I won't die! Two days go by so quickly." But I was still worried about the possible complications. Ah! What a burden friendship really is!

X lives in what was once an abbey, perched on the summit of a peak. But why, on this sweep of tranquil plains, where the earth shows no other evidence of its convulsions—why has this peak erupted from the ground, this enormous and paradoxical, solitary cone? The bizarre destiny of my friend, by some inexplicable irony, led him to this unnatural landscape, the likes of which you may never find elsewhere. The land itself seems melancholy enough to me. Of the abbey, nothing remains but a kind of house, or rather an orangery, long and low. It was a Louis XIV-era addition to the main building, of which four crumbling walls, propped up by a thick growth of ivy, are all that remain. In spite of its seclusion and the feral state its owner leaves it in, the house is charming, with its high windows, its wide front stairs, and its mansard roof, decorated with strangely green moss. All around, there are open lawns latticed with walkways of linden trees, beds blooming with wildflowers, cisterns opening in the brush like deep and grey-green eyes; terraces shaded by bowers and tall trees, huge stands of them making rows of columns in the sky, pushing up vaulted gothic skyways that open onto splendid passages to the infinite. One feels lost in that sky, sucked into that sky, immense and rough like a sea, a fantastic sky where monstrous forms, maddening fauna, indescribable flora, and nightmarish architectures evolve, wander, and disappear, endlessly. To escape this all-encompassing illusion of a sky that surrounds you with silent eternity, to see the living and mortal earth, you have to go to the edge of the terraces; you have to practically lean over them. At the foot of the peak flows a river crossed by a dam that the turbulent water fringes with foam. Two locks sleep in their basins of stone; two barges are moored on the pier. The towing path is dotted with houses and sheds that only appear from here as flat, pink roofs. And beyond the river, the plains stretch away, plains and plains and more plains, undulating with tiny dips, and tiny simple villages, hardly visible, with awkward churches, childish, the villages and their churches lost like larks' nests. On the horizon, thin strokes suggest forests. But your eyes can only descend from the celestial terraces, can only reach the earthly landscape, through the vertigo of the abyss.

Ah! What a joy it was for my friend when I, breathless from having climbed the peak in the sun—that endless peak—arrived in his strange domain! And how he had changed! He was an old man, a little old man, scrawny and stooped, and his eyes were confused and haunted, shifting like the sky they reflected. He looked at me for a long time, took my hands, wept, and could only stammer:

"Ah! It's you. It's you! I'm happy, so happy . . . "

We sat down on a stone bench. To cut off my friend's effusions, which were starting to get on my nerves, I exclaimed:

"What a charming place!"

He grabbed my arm and cried, "Don't say that . . . don't look at it!"

"Don't look at what?" I asked in surprise.

"The sky. Oh, the sky! You don't know how it crushes me, how it's killing me. It mustn't kill you too . . . "

He stood up:

"Let's go down by the lock. We can eat at an inn. I wouldn't have wanted you to come to this place, but I have no one here . . . I have nothing here. Let's go down to the inn. There are people talking down there, people living! Here no one speaks, no one lives. No one ever comes here . . . because of that sky."

My friend's words and the eerie, staccato way he spat them out made me draw back instinctively, and he said:

"No . . . you can't understand yet . . . "

He pointed to the sky with a fearful gesture, and said gravely:

"Look, you don't mess around with the sky! Now let's go down to the inn."

Chapter II

Despite this off-puttingly weird reception, and although I was tired after the long trip and my painful climb up the mountainside in the sun, I didn't dare insist upon remaining in that delicious retreat. There was such crushing suffering in my friend's eyes, such a painful look of bewilderment!

"Fine, let's go," I said. "We'll go to the inn if that's what you want."

"Yes, yes, that's it," cried X. "If you only knew how good it is inside the inn. It's nice and dark!"

I got up and took my bag.

"Come on, let's go . . . "

I grumbled to myself, sorry to have obeyed an impulse of absurd generosity, to have let myself be so easily duped by the specter of pity, the stubborn wraith that returns whenever your guard is down, forcing its way into even the most love-proof hearts. And what was going to happen to me, with this lunatic? The word "inn" evoked images of crime. No, I was really not reassured. I felt like I'd just fallen stupidly into a trap. Indeed, it had been fifteen years since I'd really known anything about X. His letters? But there's only hypocrisy and deceit in letters. I looked at X, trying to see to the bottom of him, to understand his bizarre tics. I almost felt sorry for him. He was trembling under the glare of the sky like a hare that feels the hound's breath as it pounces.

"Shall we go?" I said in a slightly irritated voice.

We went back down the mountainside.

Its inclines were worn down and slippery, and pebbles rolled under our feet. A narrow goat trail wound its way around the peak, tracing thin meanders through the short and greyish verdure. A stunted, sickly flora—a few pale orchids and crumpled little poppies, some meager thistles—grew here and there, above chewed-off grasses and brambles with their dry stalks creeping over the ground like dead blind-worms. The closer we got to the plain below, as the earth seemed to rise into the sky and invade it, as the sky over our heads retracted its diminishing vault, the more X calmed down and relaxed; you could say his physiognomy became more human. Even his shaggy beard was brightened by a smile. He said in a soft voice:

"Oh, you're so good to have come. Think how long it's been since I've seen anyone. And I feel like I have so many things to tell you, things that have been building up for fifteen years . . . I'm sick from it, I would have died."

"Couldn't you have told me up there?" I said reproachfully.

"Up there? No, no, I couldn't. Up there it's suffocating, my limbs give way, it's like there's a mountain sitting on my skull! It's the sky! It's so, so heavy! And then there are those clouds. Haven't you seen them? Wan and leaden and grimacing like a fever . . . like death!"

"You're sick," I said.

"No, I'm not sick. Why would I be sick? Up there, the air is pure. It's gone through the forests and over the plains. It's been filtered through the trees and flowers. I'm all alone . . . and by myself, however impure I may be, I can't poison all that air. No, I'm not sick."

"OK, so you're bored. So why stay here?"

"Where should I go? I have no money. I've got just enough to live on. And anyway I'm not bored. It's not that; it's something else. I think I'd be perfectly happy if it weren't for the sky. The sky frightens everyone. As soon as someone goes up there, the vertigo hits him. With nothing but the sky, nothing but the void all around you . . . There's never solid ground, never anything tangible and familiar to rest your eyes on. So right away, everyone wants to leave. I had a little maid . . . she was pretty. There are times, you understand, when a man needs . . . "

I smirked, and my friend added:

"No, no, it's not what you're thinking. God, no! I just want to see beauty around me, living beauty . . . earthly beauty! Eyes, a mouth, the curve of a waist, hands that move, hair rippling in the sun. To hear the rustling of a dress, cheerful laughter, words as sweet as songs! . . . Well, she took off. Chased off, by the sky, by those clouds. And since then, no one has ever come back. I had a dog too. One night he started barking and didn't stop till dawn. The next day, when I came out to see him and talk to him, I saw that he'd broken his chain and run away too. Would you believe there's not even a bird up there? Nothing but moles. Damn it, it's too obvious. You understand that . . .

His incoherence was tiresome. I tried to change the subject of this demented conversation: "Are you still working, at least?" I interrupted. "You used to have some talent."

"Well I . . . that is to say . . . I had been working. I jotted down my reactions . . . all the thoughts that were running around in my head. But what do you want? I haven't got so much as a book; I have nobody. I have no idea what's going on in the world besides what I've heard from the bargemen and a few issues of *Le Petit Journal* that people left on tables in the inn."

"All the more reason that the stuff you write should be good . . . or at least original."

"I'm afraid my stuff is a little bit crazy, actually . . . But if you want, I'll give you my notes. You can take them and read them . . . "

"And why don't you write more?"

"I don't have time. I don't have the time anymore. Every morning, I go down to the lock and I either spend the day walking on the piers or drinking with the sailors. I've even found something I like to do. When a stranger comes to the lock, I go up to him and say: 'You, sir, have no doubt come to visit the abbey. It's the only interesting thing around here . . . such beautiful architecture.' And then I make him climb up the peak with me. But we get very few strangers . . . ."

So," I said, laughing, "you just screw with people."

"No, I don't do it to be funny. I do it so I can be with someone, talk with someone, find things out. Except that so far, I've only met idiots who all say the same thing: 'Beautiful view! But it's too bad there's haze. You can't see things clearly enough.'"

We had arrived at the pier. It was deserted. On one of the barges, a woman was hanging laundry, a man was pumping water and making strange faces . . . and you could hear the water roiling against the dam.

We entered the only inn. Bellowing voices, smoke, a strong smell of alcohol and sour drinks, rancid butter, and acrid fried food.

"Come this way," said X, pulling me by the sleeve of my jacket.

I found myself seated in a dark room among tables of sailors in front of glasses of brandy, smoking and drinking. Their faces were black from coal and they wore greasy smocks, pounding their large gnarled hands on the tables, making the glasses shake. You couldn't hear anything but the fists pounding, the glasses tinkling, and their thick voices, bitterly spitting out "By God!"

"It's nice here, isn't it?" said X, his face shining again with joy.

He seemed to enjoy wallowing in the stench of this hovel. On a folding table we were served unmentionable stews that I refused to touch.

"Nice here, isn't it? my friend repeated, eating and drinking greedily.

In the evening, I had to bring him back drunk to the abbey. His soft and scrawny body floated in my arms like a rag ...

Chapter III

I spent a terrible night there, unable to get a moment's sleep. Heavy storm clouds, fringed by the pale light of the moon, rolled by in the sky; a suffocating heat clogged my lungs, made my breathing painful and labored. My head felt heavy, my stomach too, and my legs trembled, weak with dizziness. Was it fever? Was it hunger? I hadn't eaten since the morning. My ears were filled with strange sounds, like distant bells ringing or wasps buzzing, a trumpet choir surrounding me with its obscure melody. I didn't want to get undressed, so I lay fully clothed on the bed, a squalid bed whose blanket and sheets exhaled mildew and the stench of cadavers. Oh! That room. Its dirty, bare walls were streaked with runny yellow saltpeter, hideously crawling with black insects and larvae; countless spider webs hung from the corners and swayed from the beams. I expected to suddenly see owls and bats gliding over my head. I felt oppressed by the vague dread one feels in haunted houses, by the unspeakable menace of a place of murder.

And then the wind came up, a furious wind that howled in the night like a pack of wolves on the hunt. The scene was all set now. The house creaked, shaken from top to bottom, so much that the walls around me seemed to sway like pendulums, floating and snapping like soft draperies. Fear gripped me. I thought I heard sinister cries, the clamoring of a crowd, beasts caterwauling, demons laughing, the death rattles of slaughtered animals, all penetrating my sinister foxhole through the window-joints and the cracks in the doors. The flickering candlelight cast outsized, leering shadows on the ceiling and walls.

I got up from the bed and paced around the room . . .

"I should have expected all of this," I told myself. Meanwhile, to drive away the fear that was starting to get the best of me, I thought how different my apartment in Paris was—so intimate, so quiet, so full of consoling and charming things. Oh, nostalgia is such a stupid thing! And how he'd tricked me! Was X so important to me? I had erased him from my life! Why would I need to see this hayseed again? I remembered his letters—"I have so many things to tell you!" he would write to me. "So many things that are suffocating me!" But all he did was spout nonsense and get drunk! You can try to get as worldly wise as you like, we're always prey to the stupidity of sentiment. Let's just hope that he doesn't try to borrow money! Maybe he's nothing but a lousy mooch! He wants money? That's not going to happen! While we were climbing back up here, why didn't I just let him slide down the mountain?

The mental image of the poor bastard rolling down the steep pitch, smashing his head and breaking his arms and legs on the rocks below, did not horrify me.

"That would have been better for him," I thought, as though it were the most natural thing in the world. "There's probably no one who's even interested in him. Neither the sailors down below nor the moles here in the sky would have asked about him. When a man falls into this state of madness and degradation, he's better off dead. What will become of him? One fine morning they'll find him eaten by the spiders and the rats! No, really, I would be doing him a first-class favor."

I was satisfied by this idea for a while; it seemed to relieve my anger and disappointment, and I speculated, "It's amazing that there aren't more useless and annoying people who disappear that way! Life offers us so many opportunities at every instant!"

But then my mind wandered over a thousand confused images of a thousand half-memories, a thousand vague landscapes, faded out like old tapestries. I remembered my friend's good face, so kind, always ready to smile, with eyes like a devoted dog, and his back—his poor back—which his precocious bad luck seemed to have bent so young under the weight of misfortunes he couldn't escape. Even his clumsy way of moving marked him as an unlucky man—and I was seized by pity again for this poor creature, marked from his youth with the terrible sign of predestined sorrows.

"After all . . . he's just a poor devil!"

I suddenly recalled that X had kept a mistress, the only lover I've known him to have. A little tobacco seller, dark featured, very pale, and very dirty, whom he loved as madly as he did everything he loved. I took his mistress from him. Not because I loved her or even because I thought she was pretty, but to experience the joy, so rare and strong, that you feel when you make a loyal friend suffer, and when you know he will never complain. He forgave me, stupidly and clumsily, his voice shaking as he sobbed.

"No! No! I'm not mad at you. I didn't know that you loved her! I couldn't know. If I had known, if only I'd known!"

How he bawled! How ridiculous and repulsive he was!

I don't know why, but just having this memory almost felt like remorse. That dark-haired, pale, dirty little woman might have been the only joy he'd ever had! Maybe I had even come here to absolve myself of that horrible cowardly act.

Outside the wind redoubled its fury. I could clearly hear the trees smashing their branches together, the blowing leaves growling like organ pipes; I could hear the shingles peel from the roof, whistle through the air, and fall to the ground . . .

"Poor devil!" I said again.

The night seemed very long to me. The wind didn't subside till morning, when the sun rose into a freshly cleared and tranquil sky. I went down to the garden. The new, crisp air comforted me; I filled my lungs completely with it, and, though there was no water, I washed my face with the dew that dripped from the trees and rose from the grass, deliciously fresh.

After a short stroll, I found my friend sitting on the stone bench with his head in his hands.

"Come over here," he said to me, shifting over a little to make a spot for me beside him.

He was ashen, with swollen red eyelids. His beard was still streaked with the previous evening's debris, not to mention the night's vomit. He addressed me with a thick, pasty voice that carried his fetid breath to my nostrils:

"I can see you're disgusted by me, and that you're going to leave. I wanted to tell you some things ... some things ... but I'm still drunk. And anyway I can't talk anymore, or explain myself ... you know what I mean ... "

"So why do you get yourself worked up like this?" I asked him.

"Because I need it. You know ... Without it, I wouldn't be living—do you understand? Look ... "

He pulled a roll of greasy papers from his pocket and handed it to me.

"You can read what I wanted to tell you here in these pages. Do you get me? And when you've read them you'll burn them. It's not much, but this will explain to you ... Do you understand?"

He stammered out some more words that I didn't understand. Then he got up and said, "Good-bye! I ask your forgiveness. I believed ... that this might bring me joy ... that I might have been able to ... You understand. Good-bye!"

A few minutes later I left the hill, feeling disturbed, ambivalent, and unable to define the feelings that troubled me. I got back to Paris the same evening, and I read the following pages.

Chapter IV

I was born with the fatal gift of acute feeling, of sensitivity to the point of suffering, to the point of being ridiculous. From my earliest childhood, I imagined I saw eternal forms and strange movements in the least object, the smallest, inert thing. I used my father, my mother, my sisters and aunts to store up incredible and precocious observations. By the time I was ten I no longer cared about anything, because everything seemed crude, false, and disgusting to me. Others would have gone on to turn these traits to their advantage in commerce, finance, politics, or literature; but I did nothing with them but suffer, and they were a constant burden. My hypersensitivity came with a temper so timid that I didn't dare talk about it to anyone, not even my father—not even to my father's old dog Tom, as sweet and loyal as he was! I kept everything for myself and inside myself; I hardly even answered when people asked me questions, even if they were about the most insignificant things in the world. Often I answered only with the tears that fell from my eyes for no apparent reason. When my father asked me (he only asked me the kind of things you would ask a pet), "Did you sleep well last night?" I sobbed until I was out of breath and suffocating. It surprised my father, a wise and practical man, greatly. This interminable silence, punctuated from time to time by these inexplicable tears, made me seem incurably stupid. Though deep down I was a prodigy, I was taken for a perfect imbecile. I wound up being ill-treated by my parents as well as my teachers, who would wave their arms in theatrical frustration and say, "Nothing will ever come of this blockhead. He understands nothing and feels nothing. How unfortunate that he's an idiot!" My sisters, sweet paragons of virtue that they were, would pinch me on the sly and call me "Idiot!" with a laugh that I can still hear to this day.

On the whole, I had no luck. I grew up in an environment totally at odds with my nascent feelings and instincts, and I could never love anyone. No doubt, somewhere there exist formidable, majestic beings, endowed with intelligence, with goodness, who can inspire love in men's souls. But I have never encountered such creatures, I who by my nature was disposed to love too much and love too many. It is true that, apart from passers-by, who seemed no more meaningful to me as human beings than the pebbles on the road or the grass on the hillside, I have met very few people in my life. Since it was impossible for me to feel love for anyone, I faked it, thinking this was the way to drain the excess tenderness churning inside me. In spite of my timidity, I put on a show of enthusiasm and effusions, crazed embraces that distracted and mollified me for the moment. But onanism can't dampen the generative desires; in fact it overexcites them, turning them to insatiability. Everyone said of me: "He may be stupid, but he's so good, so tender, so devoted. He loves you so!"

I still laugh at that. Yes, even today, I enjoy a moral satisfaction and a genuine pride at the thought that I fooled everyone, including friends later on who were very proud of their supposed knowledge of psychology, the poor souls, and thought I was their guinea pig. And I think with regret that if I had applied my faculties to expressing, through dialogues with myself, the strange and ludicrous sensations that I owe to my sensibility, I could have become a comic author of the highest order. The idea never occurred to me. No idea ever occurs to me. That's been the cause of all my troubles.

Of my childhood, of my family, of that sacred nostalgia of yesteryear that is said to flavor your entire life, I have nothing but ridiculous memories. If I think about it, only a single memory remains of all my first years; I cannot resist the desire to describe it.

I had an aunt, a very ugly old maid, who lived with us. Like my sisters, every time I passed by her, she would pinch my arm for no reason and call me "Idiot!" But she was generous. On Christmas and New Year's Day, she would give me sumptuous gifts that I couldn't use. One year she gave me a flute, another year a cornet. I would have liked to know how to play these pretty instruments. But that was not in line with my father's thinking; he considered music a pastime for the lazy. My father had all sorts of considered views on education. The flute in its green velvet case and the cornet in its box of varnished wood were relegated to a closet under lock and key, and I wasn't even allowed the childish pleasure of making an untutored racket with these useless instruments. But my aunt held her ground. The following year, I received a drum; it was a real drum, with genuine skin in a beautiful copper case. My father stood musing before the drum, saying: "Well, I don't know. It might be useful. It can be good to know how to play a drum. You'll learn the drum!"

At it happens, our neighbor, the carpenter, had been a regimental drummer. He was an upstanding man who kept the faith with his former duties. For two hours every Sunday, he would bang his drum furiously to keep in practice, as he said. It also brought back glorious memories, as he had taken part in the Crimean campaign. And he punctuated his marches and drum rolls with terrible stories of the Russians: "Once, in Sebastopol, in the trenches . . . Bam, boom! Bam, bam, bam!" You could hear him from some distance. On those days, there was always a crowd in his shop.

My father got together with the carpenter and they decided the latter would be my drumming teacher. I found this decision a bit humiliating for me and profoundly ridiculous on my father's part. And when he explained to me all the advantages of learning how to play, I dissolved in tears, but he was used to my crying and paid no attention to it. Again he repeated: "You never know. One day it might prove useful. If I had known how to play the drum, well . . . " This reasoning left me unconvinced, since my father stopped in the middle of his sentence, which had taken on the mysterious tone of a confession, and I never found out what would have happened if my father had learned to play the drum. This scene ended in an outburst of tenderness. I hugged my father, who seemed convinced of my affectionate resignation: "Yes, you're not a bad boy. You're a good boy. Later on you'll understand the sacrifices I'm making for your education."

Nonetheless, I hazarded to observe: "I would have preferred the flute . . . "

But my father proclaimed: "The flute . . . that's not the same thing."

So I learned to drum. In a few weeks I became quite skilled. The carpenter was surprised and delighted with my extraordinary talent for such a, as he put it, fine and "difficult" art.

"It took me more than four months to sound a decent call to arms," he'd say. "Now, let's hear the retreat!"

Rum pumpum! Rumpa pum pum!

"Yes, you've got it! Although in the field, the drum sounds even finer, with bullets and shells flying by. You can't let your hands get cold. You see, one night in Sebastopol, in the trenches . . . "

Rum pumpum! Rumpa . . .

My father was right. You never know where the drum will take you. Drumsticks are sometimes as magical as fairy wands. Soon I felt their strange power.

In four months' time, I had become my family's pride and joy. My aunt and my sisters no longer pinched me or called me an idiot. Now, in their eyes, there was a look of admiration and respect for me. My father had become deferential. If someone came to the house, they enthused about my talent on the drum.

"Come on, little one, play the drum for us."

And in the looks they exchanged, I could read this dialogue clearly:

—You're lucky to have a child who gives you so much satisfaction.

—Yes, it's true. I have been repaid for my pains.

In the same town where I'd been taken for an incorrigible dunce, I was now considered an up-and-coming star. I flattered the vanity of my fellow citizens. They pointed me out to visitors, saying, "There's that young man who plays the drum so well."

My father, proud of all these homages, would say over and over:

"Do you see? When I told you . . . "

You should always listen to your parents.

The day was approaching when, thanks to this magical drum, I was to be invested with the only great honor that would ever, just for a moment, distinguish my life.

Chapter V

Saint Latuin was the patron saint of our parish. He was the first bishop of Normandy, in the first century of the Christian era. He beat the druids and their human blood sacrifices out of Percheron country with his staff. In very old and sincere books people wrote tales of how his shadow alone cured the sick and brought the dead to life. But he had powers yet more strange and wonderful than that. It's all a bit blurred in my memory, though. Anyway, without doubt he was a great saint, and there were few like him in all of Christianity.

The cathedral of the diocese jealously guarded a few authentic, dusty remains of this magical Saint Latuin, locked up in a reliquary of gilded bronze. In our parish, Latuin's cult was still greatly honored, kept close to our hearts by the local priest's learned scriptural exegesis. Unfortunately, all the parish had to represent its venerated patron was a crude, amorphous plaster image, indecently decayed and so generally unfit that the old people of the country recalled that when they were young the same image had also been used to represent Saint Peter and Saint Roch as needed. These various manifestations of the numinous were of course not miraculous, but rather truly undignified, and could serve as fodder for the blasphemous drolleries of the enemies of the Faith. This rankled the priest. By way of some plotting and bureaucratic maneuvers, he finally got the bishop to cough up the reliquary and give it to the parish as a gift. One Sunday morning during mass this announcement made a joyous splash, and straightaway we prepared to celebrate the transfer of the long-coveted relics with an unforgettable festival.

A singular personality named Monsieur Sosthenes Martinot lived in the area. I can still see him—big, chubby, with unctuous gestures and equally greasy smiles that squeezed through his sly lips like oil through a press; his head was bald, red, and sunken flat like an overripe tomato. He muttered under his breath like a priest at Mass.

Once a notary, M. Martinot was sentenced to six years in prison for various thefts and abuses of trust, embezzlement, and fraud. When his punishment ended and he'd resettled himself in his house, he quickly won back everyone's esteem through a shrewd piety. As he returned to social life, nobody treated him with coldness or distrust. The most honorable families received him like an old friend coming back from a long voyage. He himself spoke of his absence with a calm, distant air.

People respected him highly.

And such talent!

No one knew better than he did how to organize a religious festival, stage a procession, or decorate a repository. With his poetic imagination he was the heart of all the holidays, and the hymns he composed specially for the liturgies rapidly became popular. We would sing them not only in church but at home with our families, at vigil meals as we ate chestnuts washed down with sweet cider. M. Sosthenes Martinot was, naturally, charged with putting together the festival in honor of Saint Latuin. I dare say, this was admirable.

He came to the house one morning and said to my father:

"Can I borrow George? I need George. Yes, I think that George could lead the procession with his drum. He's not big yet—he's not a drum major—but he plays well. He plays with an extraordinary style, for his age, and this is an honor that I'd like to reserve for him."

He clasped his hands like a saint in prayer and continued:

"What a feast, my dear friend! Six arcs de triomphe— what do you think of that? I already have the whole plan, in every detail, in my head. The procession, led by George, will go to meet the bishop with the holy relics along the way, at the Moulin-Neuf. The retirees' band will play the marches I've written, and a chorus of young girls bearing golden palm leaves will sing the hymns I've composed. A group of druids in chains!—and the banners! And this, that, and the other thing!" He waved his arms.

"It will be beautiful, like a cavalcade. Would you like me to sing you the central hymn?"

Without waiting for a response, M. Martinot began to sing out of tune:

In long gone times, some horrible Gods
Reigned all over our mountains
And we Christians, in our fields,
Trembled in their hateful yoke
Oh, tender Father,
Who can make the skies
More kind?
Saint Latuin, it shall be you,
It shall be you!
St. Latuin, praiiiiise to yooou!
Jesus, my Lord, he gave you victory;
Jesus, my Lord, hath received you in his glory!
Saint Latuin, oh you we praise,
Great saint, we praise!
Saint Latuin, for us please pray!
For uuuuus please prraaaay!

My father was delighted. He thanked M. Martinot profusely.

When my father gave me the news, I cried very loudly.

"I couldn't ... never!" I stammered. It wasn't that I didn't think I could actually do it; rather, I felt acutely the absolute ridiculousness of what I was about to be plunged into.

"We can do whatever we want," my father pronounced heroically. "Work hard and apply yourself. Think of it, a procession like that, a special festival, and you leading the way—and you cry? What, you don't realize what an honor this is for you? Don't you want to make your family proud? For God's sake! A chance like this has never come my way!"

My mother, my sisters, and my aunt argued with me, shaming my feebleness. My aunt, especially, was particularly fanatical.

"If you don't want to," she screamed, "just listen. I'll take back your drum, and give it to the poor!"

"That's right, that's right," the whole family chorused, "we'll take back his drum!"

I gave up. Every day for a month, I slaved miserably away at my drum, under the eye of the carpenter who, peeved that M. Martinot hadn't chosen him, constantly repeated: "Well, isn't that a pity—a kid like this! A trifling brat! Such a little monster—and me, I was at Sebastopol!"

The big day finally arrived. The little town was strangely, feverishly animated. The streets were decked with flags, the streets and sidewalks strewn with flowers. Enormous arches of greenery, linked together by corridors of fir trees, lent to the sky, the horizon, the houses, and to all of nature an impressive aura of mystery, triumph, and joy.

At the appointed hour, the procession started off, with me and my drum leading the way. I was bizarrely decked out in a sort of sailor's overcoat with a hood lined in red wool. M. Martinot fancied the hood to be a military touch that went well with the drum. It was raining a little. The sky was all grey.

"Come on," Martinot yelled. "Give it some guts! Look sharp!"

From that point on, my memories of that infamous trek get foggy. I remember that an immense sadness came over me. Everything seemed miserable and insane. I would have liked to escape, hide, disappear, for the ground to swallow me, but M. Martinot harried me on, always behind me, with his "Look alive! Play harder! We can't hear anything!"

The rain was loosening the drum's skin, so as I pounded my sticks ever faster, it just made sad, suffocated sounds . . .

I didn't see the bishop. I didn't see the reliquary. I saw nothing; nothing but a big vague mass wherein strange figures moved, incessantly passing by and disappearing again. I heard nothing, nothing but the muddled buzz of faraway voices, of subterranean voices. I saw and heard only M. Martinot, the red scalp of M. Martinot, conducting the orchestra, herding along the druids in their chains, and leading the choir of girls, singing:

In long gone times, some horrible Gods . . .

And I beat my drum, at first mechanically, then with fury, with frenzy, carried away by a sort of hysterical madness, by a vertigo that drowned my consciousness.

This went on forever, it lasted a century, through the roads and the chapels, among the phantoms . . .

In the evening, the priest threw a grand dinner. I was presented to the bishop.

"Here is the little boy who played his drum so well, Monsignor!" said the priest, giving me a friendly tap on the cheek.

"Oh, really?" the bishop cried. "But he's so little," and

he too patted me on the cheek. The grand vicar did the same as the bishop, and all the guests, more than twenty of them, followed the Grand Vicar's cue.

"Look at you!" said my father, beaming with joy. "Will you listen to me next time?"

Since I did not respond, he added harshly, "Tsk— you don't even deserve what you've gotten!"

The following morning I came down with a fever. Meningitis trapped me between life and death for a long time, in the most awful delirium. Unfortunately, I didn't die.

And so my life began.

Chapter VI

The sickness sort of melted my brain; when I tilted my head, I felt like a liquid was sloshing back and forth against the walls of my skull, like it was being shaken up in a bottle. All of my mental processes were on hold at a way station in the middle of nothingness. I lived in the void, suspended and cradled in infinity, without any point of contact with the Earth. I remained for a long time in a state of physical numbness and a deep, soft intellectual slumber, like death.

On the doctor's advice, my parents, anxious and ashamed of me, left me in peace. I dropped the drum lessons, as well as all of my other insuperably tiring tutoring. It was for me a period of absolute happiness, of which I've never been fully conscious until now, and only in memory. For more than a year I savored—the pleasures I have now can't compare!—the immense, immense joy of not thinking anything. Stretched out on a chaise longue, eyes always closed to the light, it felt like I had found eternal rest inside my coffin. But on children's wounds, the flesh grows back quickly; the broken bones re-stitch themselves, young organs promptly recover from the jolts they receive; my life soon crashed over the obstacles that for a moment had halted the churning torrent of its juices.

My strength returned, and with it I was once again prey to my family's program for educating me, with all its baggage: the distortion of the sensibility, wounds that would never heal, and futile extravagances. Yet I got my father to let me give up the drum lessons, and the drum, despite those few hours of glory—fast forgotten —that it had granted my family, was relegated, with the flute and the trumpet, to the sepulchral darkness of an old wooden box.

From then on, every day and almost every hour, I overheard my father, my mother, my sisters, my aunt, and my tutors, all talking about what I had done and what I had failed to do, sounding half annoyed and half full of pity.

"It's so depressing...he doesn't understand a thing... he'll never understand anything. That meningitis was such a tragedy for us!" And during our silent meals, they looked on with dread as I ate, but didn't dare reproach me (oh, they were good and honest people, in the legal sense) for the morsels that I greedily devoured, and for which they knew they would never be repaid!

Instead of being diminished by the sickness that had caressed my very marrow, my sensitivity grew even greater, inflating itself till I trembled from nerves. Everything caused me suffering, for I no longer had that sense, so egotistical and reassuring, that there is beauty scattered through things, the beauty that, alone, suffices to explain, and to excuse, this mistake, this crime: the universe.

I'm not sure what I was looking for, but I looked into men's eyes, into the buds of flowers—into all the mutable and innumerable forms that life takes on—and I groaned at my failure to find anything to fit the vague, cryptic, painful, and overwhelming need that filled my heart, swelled in my veins, held all of my flesh and my soul up for impossible caresses and embraces that could not be.

One night when I couldn't sleep, I opened my bedroom window and, leaning my elbow out on the guardrail, I looked up at the sky, above a yard drowned in shadow. The sky was violet, with millions of sparkling stars. For the first time, I was conscious of that incredible immenseness; I tried to sound its depths with the meager eyes of a child, and it crushed me. Like Pascal, "The eternal silence of those infinite spaces frightened me." I felt the terror of those mute stars, whose pale flicker grows ever more distant yet never sheds light on the maddening mystery of the immeasurable. Who was I, so small, among all these worlds? Who had caused my birth, and why? And where was I going, a lowly wisp of straw, lost in this whirlwind of incomprehensible harmonies? Of what significance was I? And what were my father, my mother, my sisters, our neighbors, our friends, all these atoms carried by who knows what, to who knows where?—picked up and pushed into space, like bits of dust in the draft of a powerful, invisible broom? I hadn't read Pascal—I hadn't read anything yet—but later, when I first came across that passage I now cite from memory, I quivered with pain and joy to see them printed so concisely, so completely, those same feelings that had stirred me on that night . . .

"I don't know who sent me into this world. I don't even know what the world is, nor what I am. I'm prodigiously ignorant of everything. I don't know what my body is, nor my senses, nor my soul; and that same part of me that's thinking these words, and which reflects upon everything and upon itself, knows no more of itself than it does about everything else. I see these terrifying spaces of the universe surrounding me, and I find myself attached to a corner of this vast expanse, without knowing why I was put in this place instead of another, or why the little time I'm given to live is assigned to me just at this time rather than that, when there's an eternity that precedes my life and another that will follow. I see only infinities in every direction, which swallow me like an atom, like a shadow that lasts only an instant and can never return . . . "

All night long I stayed transfixed with my elbow leaning on the open window, never moving, my gaze lost in the terror of the sky, with my throat clenched so tight that the sobs it trapped in my chest were suffocating me. But finally the morning dawned; the sun rose, and with it came life, chasing away dreams of death. Doors opened, shutters banged against the walls; a magpie flew out of a clump of privet shrubs; the cats, leaping about in the grass, returned from their nightly hunt. I saw the maid sweeping the doorstep of our house; I saw my elder sister carry her cage of canaries out to a little table in the yard and set to work, cleaning it out and changing the water in the bowls. The canaries chirped, and my sister replied in a peevish voice; even in moments of tenderness, she spoke in a nasty little bark. From the window where I watched, my sister was hideous. Her surly silhouette, in a rumpled nightgown and dirty cap, clashed with the pure, fresh morning. Her black slip, barely clinging to her hips, sagged unpleasantly onto dirty old slippers that she dragged along the path like horrible toads. She had a mean-looking neck, the hard, dry profile of an old maid, and a mulish head. I don't know why but she annoyed me more than usual. I would have liked to beat her. I wanted to use a hammer to fill that skull with a bit of the brightness of the pristine morning. I went down to the yard and ran toward her, almost menacing. I grabbed her arm and cried:

"Silly moron idiot! You'd do better to watch the stars at night!'

My sister let out a cry, frightened by my voice and the look in my eyes, and she ran off yelling "Help!"

That same day I went with my father to the funeral of an old farmer who I didn't know. At the cemetery, as the mourners filed past the grave, I was overtaken by a strange sadness. I fled the crowd of people, who were jostling each other and fighting over the holy water, and I ran around the graveyard stumbling over the tombstones, weeping so I could have broken a gravedigger's heart. My father caught up to me.

"Good grief. What's with you? What are you crying for? Why are you running away?"

"I don't know! I can't . . . "

My dad took me by the hand and brought me back home. "Look here," he reasoned. "Did you know old Julien?"

"No."

"Therefore you didn't love him, did you?"

"No."

"So if he dies it can't cause you any pain, right?"

"No."

"So, what is it that's gotten into you? Why are you crying?"

"I don't know . . . "

After a silence, my father added, with a more severe voice, "This was not a nice thing to do. I don't know what you'll come up with next to humiliate me! I am not very happy with you. This morning you were saying who-knows-what to your sister. Now you're crying over nothing. If you keep it up, I'll never take you anywhere again . . . "

Chapter VII

It was during that time that a great change took place in our existence.

My parents decided they felt cramped in our little house, so they bought a larger property which they'd been coveting for a long time. It had an iron fence, very old trees, an arbor, an orchard, and, among the collapsed rock gardens, the remains of an old fountain. From the road the residence, all in white with a high slate roof, looked imposing to passers-by—almost lordly, as my sisters would say. Indeed, to the neighbors this home put us a notch above the no-account petit bourgeois. My sisters took on more lofty airs, and they already played ridiculously at being great ladies. They hoped also—a hope the entire family wholeheartedly shared—that the prestigious estate would help them find presentable husbands.

But all of this was not accomplished without lengthy deliberation—nor without long, fraught, harrowing waffling. For months and months we had weighed the pros and cons, raised stubborn objections, juggled the finances, measured the height of the ceilings, the width of the windows, and the depth of the cupboards;

we pounded on the walls to see if they were solid and peered through the draught of the fireplace. But it was my mother most of all who lacked, as always, the ability to make a decision.

She couldn't bring herself to make up her mind, even in the most ordinary acts, the most repetitive household matters. If she had to buy anything, from a dress to a package of turnips to a ball of thread, it was only after sighing and frowning and being goaded by necessity that she finally gave in. I still remember the indescribable negotiations she opened with a shoe-maker over the purchase of a pair of boots, negotiations that went on for two years, during which time I walked around with holes in my shoes.

So when the house was settled and the deed was signed, my mother was almost overcome by her own audacity. No! It was impossible. This irreparable reso-lution had put an end to all her obsessing, naysaying, and foot-dragging; no more "ifs," "buts," or "if-thens." It came as a violent surprise, a criminal infringement of her will, like a sudden, terrible catastrophe that no one could have prepared for. And she whimpered incessantly:

"Such a big house! And maybe it will be damp! . . . and so much land! Ah! My God, what will become of us there?"

The prospect of moving in, although long discussed and imagined in the minutest detail, overwhelmed her as if it was too great a task, the thought of which made her limbs go limp and numbed her brain. She hunted for a way to break the contract, no matter how bizarre.

"But it's signed!" said my father. "Look, you signed it yourself!"

"I've signed, I've signed, I know that," my mother replied, "but so what? Perhaps I made a mistake. There must be grounds for canceling. To begin with, I didn't sign willingly. And suppose the roof caves in tomorrow?"

"So?"

"So, I'm just telling you it's not fair . . . that we could have waited . . . and that if you really want . . . "

My father shrugged his shoulders impatiently. So she scolded him:

"Oh! You! I know. First off, you've never known the value of money . . . "

It took her several weeks to get accustomed to the fearsome idea that the transaction was irrevocable, that there was no going back, as my father explained to her, holding a copy of the law in his hand. Finally, one day, she ended up by declaring:

"After all, we've been so cramped and uneasy for so long that we can allow ourselves the pleasure of a little comfort . . . "

"Of course we can," my father chimed in. "Now you're being reasonable. My God, life is short. It's not too much to have some good times when you can . . . "

"That's true," my mother concluded, joyful and reassured. "As long as the children are happy . . . But you'll admit, all the same, that we were a bit hasty. And that big house—we'll never be able to keep it up with just our two servants."

"Of course we will. You'll take on a girl for 10 francs a month . . . "

"Well, as long as we're happy, as long as we're well!"

But from then on, my mother became serious and energetic, prowling around the house, pausing in front of every object, carrying on strange colloquies with them all.

One day at lunch, she announced gravely: "We're going to have to make some serious budget cuts. I've thought about it a lot. To begin with, there's the parlor. We don't need a parlor. We entertain so rarely. We can sell the furniture that's in the parlor."

"Oh, mother!" my elder sister said, "I thought we could make it even nicer."

"And who's paying for that? You?" My mother gave her a hard look. "Shut up . . . it's like with your piano! . . . you never play it . . . What good is a piano? Let's have no more excess. I've had enough of it!"

"But, mummy . . . you bought that piano with our savings, our little New Years' presents. If I don't play it, it's because you don't want to get the piano tuner to come and fix it. That piano is ours!"

"Nothing here is yours, do you understand?" my mother growled.

And turning to my father, who hadn't said a word:

"It's like the horse and the carriage. What do we need them for? We almost never go out. I think we could sell them. That would mean some serious savings."

"But come on," my father objected, "we can't sell everything. We didn't buy this house so we could give up everything that gives us pleasure."

The next day was even worse.

"We'll dismiss the servants," my mother declared. "The children will do the housework. I'll hire a woman by the day for the heavy chores."

Everyone gave a start. My father said:

"What? You yourself said you couldn't take care of the house with the staff that you have. That's crazy! And the garden? Have you thought of the garden? You know how I love my vegetables, my trees and fruit!"

"Your fruit! We had about twenty pears this year. I couldn't even make an apple jelly with your fruit. No, no more waste, no more clutter. You'll do for your garden the way I take care of the house: you'll hire a man by the day, one day a week."

"It's not worth the trouble of buying a bigger house if you have to sell everything and dismiss everybody."

My mother looked smug:

"Didn't I tell you? Didn't I warn you that you were doing something stupid and crazy?"

"But it was your idea to buy the house! You're the one who thought that everything was too small . . . "

"So now it's me!? I'm sorry to tell you, but you have no manners and no dignity!"

These scenes were repeated often.

It was decided that we would no longer light a lamp in the hall at night, that we would cut a course from each meal, that we would replace our wood fire with a charcoal fire, that we would keep none of our meager little luxuries, our humble pleasures.

So one morning we entered the vast, almost empty house. Public auctions had scattered our furniture, the things we were used to, and our little everyday joys to the four corners of the country.

There was nothing left but a wardrobe here and there, a chair, a table, a bed. And it was so sad—this house with its immense rooms, chilly and dour, these bare windows overlooking the unkempt lawns and the deserted avenues—so sad that I started to cry, I don't know why; the things that were gone were not that precious to me, they hadn't brought me the least bit of happiness.

And though I wept in a corner of the room where we had gathered in silence, I couldn't stop myself from savoring, along with my tears, the bitter joy of witnessing my sisters' disappointment. In their eyes I could see the death of their hopes, their suitors' escape, and their fear of eternal virginity.

Chapter VIII

These pages will not constitute an autobiography, not according to literary norms. I've lived in quiet poverty, without a single novelistic event; all my acts have been incoherent, and I'm always alone—even with family, even with old friends, even as I pass right through the middle of a crowd. I lack the vanity to suppose that the story of my life could be the least bit interesting or enjoyable to hear. So I expect this work to bring me neither glory, nor money, nor even the consolation of imagining I might tug on some rich old lady's heartstrings. The world surrounds me with its mystery, within which I am a negligible speck; no one bothers about me. And indeed, why would anyone on Earth preoccupy themselves with such a silent insect? I have, voluntarily or by accident—I don't know which—broken off all the ties that attached me to human solidarity; I have refused what little piece of the action, be it good or evil, that's doled out by chance to every living thing . . .

I don't exist in myself, nor in others, nor in the most infinitesimal rhythm of the harmony of the universe. I am that inconceivable and perhaps unique thing: nothing! I have arms, the approximation of a brain, traces of a male member, and nothing's come of it all—nothing, not even death. And if Nature persecutes me so, no doubt it's because I'm dallying too long in returning to her this little pile of compost, this pinch of rot, that is my body, and in which so many creatures—charming ones, who knows?—so many curious organisms are waiting to be born, to carry on the life with which I'm really doing nothing, nothing except to interrupt it in my cowardly way. What does it matter if I've cried, if I've drug my fingernails like a ploughshare over my bloody chest? In the midst of universal suffering, what are my tears? What does my voice mean, torn up with sobbing or laughter, in this grand lamento that shakes worlds, maddens them with the impenetrable enigma of matter and divinity?

If I have dramatised these few memories of my childhood, it wasn't so people would feel sorry for me, or admire me, or hate me. I know that I don't have the right to any of those feelings in the hearts of men. And what would I do with them? Does the voice of supreme pride speak in me now? Was I trying to explain, to excuse, with oversubtle reasoning, how the angel that I could have been was degraded into the obscene, slithering larva that I am? Oh, no! I have no pride, I have no more pride! Every time such a sentiment has penetrated me, I've had only to raise my eyes to the sky to dispel it—toward that terrifying suckhole of infinity, where I feel smaller, more unnoticed, more insignificant than an amoeba, lost in the sludgy water of a cistern. Oh, no! I swear, I have no more pride.

What I did want was to shape these memories into a life-like and familiar narrative, in order to bring to light one of the heaviest tyrannies, one of the most crushing oppressions in life, and one which I haven't been the only one to suffer, unfortunately—that is to say, paternal authority. Because everyone suffers from it, everyone carries it with them, in their eyes, on their forehead, on the back of their neck, on every part of the body where the soul reveals itself, where the emotions inside seep out in sad illumination, in odd deformations that show the characteristic and mortal signs, the terrible thumb-print, of this initial, ineffaceable family education. And also it seems that my pen, as it grinds against the paper, distracts me a bit from the terror of this silence, from the terror of my solitude, from the terror of these rafters, where something heavier than the sky in the garden weighs on my head—the terror of the night. What's more, it seems to me that as I trace these words, they become beings, living characters, characters who move, who speak, who speak to me—ah! Can you imagine the sweetness of getting what you hardly dared hope for?—they speak to me!

I loved my father, I loved my mother. I loved them even in their ridiculousness, even when they mistreated me. And in the moment of confessing this act of faith, now that they're both down below, under the lowly stones, all dissolute flesh and crawling maggots, I love them; I cherish them even more, I love and cherish them with all the respect that I have lost. I blame them neither for the misery they handed me directly, nor for the unspeakable destiny that their complete and respectable stupidity imposed upon me. They were what all parents are, and I can't forget that when they were children they no doubt suffered the same things they put me through. We hand this fatal legacy down to each other with our constant, faithful virtuousness. All the blame goes to society, for never finding any better way to legitimize its thefts or to sanctify its absolute power—most of all its power to trap man in a state of complete imbecility and total servitude—than by instituting this admirable mechanism of government: the family.

Every reasonably well-constituted being is born with some dominant faculties, some individual strengths, which correspond exactly to a need or to a pleasure in life. Instead of helping them develop normally, the family moves fast to suffocate and drown them. It produces nothing but social outcasts, rebels, unbalanced people, unhappy people, through its marvelous instinct for alienating them from themselves; by using its legal authority to impose upon them tastes, functions, and actions that aren't their own, and that become not the joy that they should be, but an intolerable martyrdom. How many people do you meet who are equal to being themselves?

I had a love, a passion, for nature, that was rare for a child my age. Everything about it interested me; everything intrigued me. How many times did I spend hours before a flower, vaguely, dimly groping for the secret and the mystery of its life? I observed the spiders, ants, and bees with a profound joy, laced with the awful anxiety of not knowing, of not understanding anything. I often asked my father questions, but he never answered them, and always made fun of me.

"You're a strange one," he told me. "Where do you find all the things you tell me about! You want to know what bees are? They're female bumblebees, like frogs are female toads . . . and they sting lazy children . . . are you happy now?"

I had no books and nobody to guide me. Nothing could discourage me, though, and my childish struggle with the incomprehensible grandeur of nature was touching.

One day they were digging a well at the house, and as young and ignorant as I was, I figured out the law of physics that they use to find artesian wells. During my daily observations I had often been struck by the way the levels of liquids in communicating vessels interact. Through this reasoning I applied the theory, though still confused and embryonic in my mind, to underground water-pockets, and I realized that water might bubble up from a spring if you drilled at the right spot in the nearby earth.

I shared this discovery with my father; I explained it to him the best I could, with a flood of words and gestures that was unusual for me.

"What are you going on about now?'" my father cried. "All you've 'discovered' is the artesian well!"

And once again his smooth face was furrowed by an ironic smile that completely humiliated me.

"I don't know," I stammered. "I . . . was asking you . . . "

"You little ass! They discovered that a long time ago . . . Ha! Ha! Ha! I bet tomorrow you'll discover the moon."

And my father burst out laughing. How that laugh hurt me!

That's when my mother butted in.

"Didn't you know?" he updated her. "We have a great man for a son. Junior here just discovered artesian wells."

"What an imbecile," my mother said. "He'd do better to learn his catechism."

Next my sisters ran up to take their turn, with their sharp, curious faces.

"Congratulate your brother! He just discovered artesian wells."

"He'll say anything to be ridiculous," they squealed, ticking out their tongues.

Soon the neighbors, our friends, and the whole countryside knew I had discovered a method for digging wells, like sticking a spoon in butter. And they surrounded my poor humiliated little person with a wave of laughter, of universal mockery. I felt the scorn of an entire village weighing on me, and I thought I would die of shame.

They decided to send me to school to teach me to live.

Chapter IX

I don't feel like saying much about my school years. Anyway, I can sum up in a word what they did to me: I was brutalized. The education I got there only worsened what my family had begun. At home, it's rare that a child doesn't feel some sort of warmth and affection, as well as a kind of familiar security, to substitute for clear ideas and notions about life. It's often a vague thing, but it still offers him a prop. Love is so powerful that even when it's stupid and mediocre it opens whole horizons of moral beauty to the soul. But at school, there's no such thing. The child is left to the indifferent, heavy hands of mercenaries with no stake in him; no personal interest, nor tenderness, nor vanity. They arrive, they hurry through, and they're gone. And I can't describe the intolerable boredom that emanates from the pack of absurdities, lies, and ridiculous diplomas that is a teacher. Instead of piquing your interest in the lessons he assigns by giving them some life and zest, the teacher makes you feel disgust, as you would for something ugly. He fills everything with his stiff, fake gravitas, a proudly stupid dogmatism that kills the curiosity in a child's soul instead of developing it. With marvelous certainty and a miraculous precision, the teacher plasters such a thick glaze of ignorance—such a corrosive slime of prejudice—over juvenile minds that it's almost impossible to ever escape them. There are some young souls that rebel against this horrible course of study in mediocrity; I admire them, but how I pity them! Are there any trials or miseries their lives won't have in store?

I remember the plaster sculpture we had on the dining room mantel; my mother had bought it from a little Italian traveling salesman, and it featured naked children playing marbles. It was hideous, but such was my mother's artistic taste. Unfortunately the flies kept leaving brownish spots on the plaster, to my family's great chagrin. My sisters, to whom the care of this work of art had been entrusted, had tried in vain to scrape them off, to wash them off, to dust them over with flour, but the embarassing stains wouldn't disappear. On the contrary, they either worked themselves deeper into the grain of the plaster, or spread further across its surface, indelible. After a few years the sculpture was completely black. They had to throw it in the trash. That fly shit made a perfect metaphor for my teachers' lessons, and I knew that my little personality was disappearing, little by little, under the daily deposits of excrement.

Ah yes, teachers. I knew a young man who had strange and incomparable memories of his teacher! He became a man of letters and dedicated books to him; he publicly and enthusiastically thanked him for awakening his soul to a multitude of beauties, for having unveiled for him the mysteries of nature. Do I need to say that I will never meet such an inconceivable deity? All that my teachers taught me was that only physical force is beautiful and enviable, and that I was weak; they taught me to revere the grossest virtues, the most craven acts, the animal passions, the superiority of brutes, and the heroism of pugilists.

I came out of school stripped of everything and perfectly disciplined. From constant discouragement I had lost my taste for inquiry and the capacity for emotion. My astonishment and enthusiasm before nature, which had once sustained my intellect at a decent level and protected me from the contagious vulgarity in which my sisters wallowed, had fallen away. I had no more desire or inspiration for great things; I was ripe to be picked for a soldier, a notary, or whatever kind of larval functionary my father might like me to become . . . I wouldn't dream of disputing his future decisions to destroy my honor.

So there were long family summits, wherein all of the social positions were held up for review. No one cared what aptitude I might have for this or that function; it was a question of the social and pecuniary advantages that each offered. The decision of these interminable secret councils—which were held without me anyway—was that nothing stood out, and that while I waited for a decision, I would work copying documents for a notary.

"It's good practice," said my father, "and it leaves your options open."

It was during this period that an extraordinary episode in my life taught me what love is about.

My aunt, as I've said, was a strange woman who didn't seem to put a lot of logical thought into what she did. One day, she was mauling me with tenderness and gifts; the next she would beat me for no reason. Everything she did seemed to come at the behest of an incomprehensible folly. Sometimes she would spend entire days shut away in her room, sad and crying, and no one knew why. And the next morning she'd be singing, caught up in noisy gaiety and preoccupied with projects. Often I saw her moving huge logs around in the woodshed, shoveling dirt around, working harder than a ditch digger. She was really ugly, so ugly that no one had ever asked for her hand in marriage; the family guessed she must be suffering dearly from being an old maid. Her veiny red face had such dry skin that it looked like a fire inside her had scorched it enough to raise scales. Her hair was short and thin, and she herself was very thin and a bit hunchbacked; my poor aunt was a truly disagreeable sight. Her sudden tenderness bothered me even more than her rages. She would kiss me furiously, with embraces so hard and brusque that I'd have rather she pinched my arms.

When I came home from the boarding school, both her fondness and her malice took a shocking turn. Sometimes after lunch, she would drag me down into the garden, running like a little girl. There was a little arbour room there, and in the room was a bench. We sat on the bench saying nothing to each other. She would pick a dead twig up off the ground, and chew on it in a rage . . . her rosacea turned a brighter shade of red and her scaly skin strained over the arc of her bones; her eyes, suddenly bloodshot, took on a strange gleam . . .

"Why aren't you talking to me?" she would ask, after several minutes of embarrassing silence.

"Uhhh, well, Auntie . . . "

"Oh, look how your tie is messed up! What a little scruff you are!"

She would then pull me close to her and rearrange the knot on my tie, her movements quick and jerky. I felt the bones of her fingers scraping my throat. Her stale breath, sour and hot, offended my nostrils. I really wanted to leave—not that I sensed any specific danger, but everything she was doing was intolerable to me. Then all at once my aunt stood up, pawed the ground impatiently, and slapped me hard in the face.

"There you go! Take that. You're a dolt. You're a little beast. A mean little beast!"

And she would dart away, stifling a sob as she ran.

One afternoon, we were sitting there on the bench in the arbour room.

"Why do you look at Mariette?" my aunt said suddenly.

Mariette was a little housemaid we had at the time.

"But I don't look at Mariette," I replied, stunned by the question.

"I'm telling you that you look at her. I don't want you looking at her. I'll tell your mother."

"But Auntie, honestly . . . " I insisted . . .

But I didn't have a chance to finish my sentence— tangled, suffocated, crushed by what felt like a thousand arms, a thousand mouths, I felt something horrible and unknown approach . . . then I was enveloped by something abominable. I fought back violently. I pushed the beast back with my teeth, my nails, my elbows—with all my strength, multiplied tenfold by my horror of her body.

"No! No! I don't want to!" I cried. "Auntie, I don't want it. I don't want to!"

"Shut up, imbecile," my aunt groaned, her lips rolling on my lips.

"No! Stop it, Auntie, stop it, or I'm calling Mama!"

The clamp relaxed, released my chest and my legs; my lips were free, to draw in a breath of fresh air, and through the branches I saw my aunt fleeing up the walk toward the house.

I didn't dare go home until dinnertime that evening, troubled by the idea of seeing my aunt.

"Your aunt left," my father said, wrinkling his forehead. "She had a discussion with your sisters and she's gone."

And he added: "Oh, I know her. She won't be back. How annoying. Three thousand francs a year gone— what a pain!"

Dinner was morose and silent. Everyone stared at the empty seat.

We never saw my aunt again; we never heard any news from her.

Oh, my poor aunt, you pitiful and anguished creature, where are you? And why didn't I give you the happiness that the whole world had refused you?

Chapter X

It's cold; the canal is frozen. Strange, still crows ride on heavy ice floes that lazily follow the current, and the canal banks resound, up and down, with the charming song of a harmonica. A black tugboat and six very black dinghies, black like they're carrying plague and death, wait for the thaw, though the water they're sitting in might be frozen solid by tomorrow; the chunks of ice press together, getting closer, piling up on each other with gentle cracking sounds. Fog covers the fields; the popple trees are now no more than a vague violet outline in the flattened landscape.

Idle sailors come and go along the pier and fill up the cabaret. You can almost smell the booze in people's eyes, and murder is on the prowl. Just now two men came out looking furious and pulled out their knives. It's sinister.

Wild ducks fly in symmetrical flocks, pinwheeling and crying in a low sky that's grey-blue above the fog, a blue touched with queasy metallic glints, and I saw a swan go by, white and bleeding, to collapse on the island behind the poplars. Ah! How white it was against that funereal blue, and how red as well! Why did they kill it? Man can't stand to let something beautiful and pure, a thing on wings, pass over him. He hates everything that soars, and everything that sings. It seemed to me that this swan is the very image of my dream, and my dream is dead.

All around, coming from everywhere, you hear rifle shots; above you, from all over, like moans, like screams. The sky is filled with death throes, just like the earth.

This evening, I came back up from the canal a bit drunk, not really wasted, but with a strange heaviness in my head. On the threshold of the cabaret, where I left the grinning men behind, a chill seized me, and the ascent from the canal bank hasn't warmed me up. Ordinarily when I've drunk too much, I fall like a lump into bed and I sleep and sleep, a happy sleep, a sleep full of parades of beautiful chimeras and consoling joys. But this evening I'm not sleepy; I've never felt as sad as I do tonight. I try in vain to recover and follow the train of my memories. I remember nothing anymore . . . it all floats in my head, like a heavy, impenetrable fog. And I'm afraid of the silence that surrounds me, I'm afraid of my shadow there on the wall, I'm afraid of that wailing dog . . . why does he only bark when I'm sad? Oh! These still nights! These dead nights, when not a breath of air comes to stir the branches of the trees, or lift the tiles of my roof, or make the windows crack—how terrible they are! I try to take refuge in the past, to recall faces and things . . . my father is dead, my mother is dead, my sisters are married . . . but this evening I can't even remember how all of that happened! . . .

Ah! Here's my companion. My only companion. It's

a little spider. She dropped from the ceiling on an invisible thread and stopped a few centimetres from the lamp's glass cover, but outside of its glow. And she rests there, her long limbs folded, at the end of the thread she just spun. Why? There are no more flies, no more insects. And she hangs there idle, doesn't spin any webs or lie in ambush. She seems to sleep, her belly turned to the warmth of the lamp. She sleeps or she dreams. A mischievous impulse makes me move the lamp to the right. So, nimble like a gymnast, the spider climbs back up the invisible thread, crosses the ceiling, and drops back down a new thread until she's set herself up again in the heat of the lamp. She refolds her long spindly legs, seesaws for an instant, and is still again. I repeat the experiment several times, pulling away the lamp, to the right, to the left, and the spider always climbs back up and back down to station herself, with an admirable precision, close to the glass with its gentle warmth. As I watch the spider, the minutes pass, the hours roll by; I watch the still little spider, and it seems that she's watching me as well, her eight eyes fixed ironically upon me; and I hear her say to me:

"You're sad, you despair, and you cry! It's your own fault. Why did you want to become a fly? You could have easily been like me, a joyful spider . . . Don't you see, in life, you have to eat or be eaten? Myself, I prefer to eat . . . and it's so amusing! The flies are so confident, so stupid. You put out a little snare, practically nothing—a few threads in the sun, between two leaves, between two flowers. The flies like the sun, they like light, they like flowers, they're all poets. They come and tangle their wings in the webs strung round those flowers in the sun . . . and you take them, and you eat them. Flies taste so good! . . . Oh, how stupid you are, go away! Your lamp is dying, good night!'

And the spider climbs back up to the ceiling and disappears behind a rafter in the shadows.

That dog is still barking outside! Another dog, farther away, answers. I feel the chill of death invade me.

I go to the window. The moon has risen and chased away the fog. Between the bare branches of the trees, the sky alights and the stars burn cruelly. And I think:

"So what if I had been a human spider, so what if I had savored the joy of murder? Would I have been happy, or happier? Would I not have been crushed anyway by the mystery of that sky, by all that's unknown, by all of this infinity that weighs on me? What does it matter if I live the way I live? Life is the only sorrow! To live in pleasure amongst the crowd, or to live in solitude, surrounded by dread and silence—aren't they the same thing? And I don't have the courage to kill myself!"

I didn't drink enough tonight . . .

Chapter XI

My sisters were set to get married in a few months. They were marrying some nondescript, strangely stupid creatures, one of whom was a tax agent; I forget what the other one did. I barely spoke a word to them, and treated them as strangers. When they figured out that I counted for nothing in the family, both of them totally ignored me, looked down at me me for my weakness, for my solitary habits, for everything in me that was not in them. They were big, oafish, noisy braggarts, having spent a lot of time in the heavy, asphyxiating air of stupidity of the little cafés in the village. There they learned and retained special, technical-looking gestures, so that when they walked, held out a hand, waved hello or ate they always seemed to be playing pool, to be putting on a backspin, making an important and difficult shot. And, naturally, they'd had all sorts of marvellous adventures in which they'd always acted the hero. In the family and in the region, everyone found them to be extremely distinguished.

"How lucky they are!" people exclaimed, envying my sisters.

The tax agent had made his debut as a functionary in a little district in the Alps. There he had hunted mountain goats, which made him an admirable and almost mysterious character. When he recounted his escapades in the mountains and on the points of precipices, where tragic torrents growled and ferried unknown corpses, acting out the scenes with grand gestures—the high peaks, the intrepid guides, the leaping goats, the rifle shots; "Bang! Bang!" and the mortally hit beast stretched out on the snowy, bloody stones—my sister was in ecstasy, climbing the pure, drunken, infinite summits of love. She gazed at him, contemplated him, as Elsa her supernatural Lohengrin!

The other one didn't hunt goats. His hobby was perhaps less noble, but it was equally marvellous and fascinating: He was obsessed with jumping over things. He'd jump any kind of obstacle. And he did it with a daring and suppleness that made my other sister's heart pound, as though her fiancé had stormed cities, routed armies, and conquered entire peoples. When we were out walking, at the sight of a barrier or a gate in the hedge he would suddenly interrupt the conversation, take off, jump across and back over the obstacle, and return to us, his cheeks redder, gasping a bit, with an air of triumph in his eyes, and he would look at us one after another, saying, "You do that!"

Then he'd turn to me: "You do as much! Try it!"

And they'd laugh mockingly, "Ha ha, him?! He doesn't know how to do anything!"

So, all day long, we'd hear the story—what an epic—of all the obstacles he'd ever jumped, barriers as big as houses, like oaks, like mountains—red, white, and green gates, walls and hedges . . . Then he would stretch out his hams, flexing them, making them dance, proud of his muscles. This sister swooned with love just like the other, transported by the heroism of his incomparable thigh, dreaming of sublime and terrible joys. Oh, but she was ugly as she grimaced! And how I pitied her! One afternoon we found them on the bench where I'd sat with my aunt, my sister half-unconscious in the arms of her fiancé, who was stretching out that admirable ham with a significant and victorious gesture. It was time to hurry up with the marriage.

And I remember horrible, repugnant scenes at night in our parlor, in the glow of the lamp whose tragic light revealed their strange faces, their insane faces, the faces of the dead.

The tax officer's mother came by once to discuss the conditions of the contract and to put the arrangements for the trousseau in order. She wanted to get everything and give nothing, arguing peevishly over each article. Her face was wrinkled with bitter folds; she flooded my sister with sharp glances and hate-filled stares as she repeated herself endlessly.

"Ah! No, no! We didn't say that! That was never under discussion! A shawl from India? What do you think we are, the royal family?"

My father, who had backed down on a lot of issues, threw a fit when the old lady contested the Indian shawl.

"Maybe we aren't the royal family, but we are decent and honorable people, and the Indian shawl was promised. You will give us the Indian shawl!"

And in a dry, uncompromising tone he added:

"I demand it! I've been able to make some sacrifices, for the happiness of these young people, but here I insist!"

He stood up and paced around the parlor, hands folded behind his back, the fingers squirming with anger. There was a moment of dramatic silence.

My mother was pale and my sister's eyes were brimming with tears, her throat clenched. The tax agent stared in embarrassment at a chrome lithograph hanging on the wall.

The old lady piped up: "And it'll do you all a lot of good for the girl to have an Indian shawl if she's got nothing to eat!"

"My daughter? Nothing to eat?" my father interrupted, planting himself directly before the old woman, almost menacing. Her face scrunched up coarsely. "And who do you take me for, Madame?"

But she was stubborn. "An Indian shawl! Think for just one minute . . . if you only knew how much that costs!"

"I don't need to know!"

My mother, growing paler and paler, said: "Madame! This is the tradition! A trousseau is a trousseau! We didn't ask for lace, even though, in our position, we could have very well have demanded a lace shawl too. But the Indian shawl! Look, this wouldn't be a serious marriage without it."

"Fine. It's still no! If you want an Indian shawl, you'll pay for it."

My sister, her eyes filled with tears, muffled a sob in her handkerchief. She hiccoughed sorrowfully. It was a poignant moment.

"My daughter!" cried my father.

"My poor baby!" cried my mother.

"Mademoiselle, mademoiselle!" cried the tax official, whose arms swung to and fro as though they were pushing a long cue stick at an enormous billiard ball . . .

Between her hiccoughs and sobs, my sister pleaded in a muffled voice, snuffling in the moist wads of her handkerchief.

"I don't want any! . . . any shawl . . . from India . . . I want to be married! I want to be married!"

They led her into her room. She let herself be dragged along, like an inanimate thing, and wouldn't stop repeating, "I want to be married! I want to be married!"

She got married, finally, without the Indian shawl; then she left. My other sister also got married, with no Indian shawl . . . then she left . . .

And I no longer heard my sisters yapping; a silence invaded the house. My father became very sad. My mother cried, not knowing what to do with the long days, and the canaries in their abandoned cage died one after another. As for myself, I copied documents for the notary, and my fascinated eye watched the parade of all the passions, all the crimes, and all the murder that the desire for a piece of land seeds in the hearts of men . . .

Chapter XII

My father and my mother died on the same day, carried away in an epidemic of cholera. My grief was so great that I don't know how to describe it. In the suddenness of the catastrophe, I forgot all the petty grudges I thought I had against my parents and gave in to tears without reserve. I had never thought that I could love them so much. Unknown feeling sleeps in a man's heart, like a miser's treasure under the earth. It only awakes to the great axe-blows of misery. And how my heart labored under those blows!

Added to my sadness was a bitter and violent remorse, the remorse of having perhaps not quite properly cared for my parents. But imagine my situation. Frightened of the illness, our maid had fled the house. There wasn't a single person around who would help me beside the sick bed. And I was alone, all alone and all weakness before that terror.

The doctor would only show his face to say, "It's getting worse, they're lost"; then he would give me a vague prescription without telling me how to use it and quickly take off, a bit pale, for other households, where his acid voice no doubt repeated that eternal sentence to other poor little creatures like myself: "It's getting worse, they're lost." I didn't even know whether the prescription was meant to be taken as a draught; I was so afraid of making some mistake that I abstained from administering such dubious medicine.

"Son!" my father cried, twisting in his bed. "I'm freezing . . . warm me up . . . I'm dying of the cold . . ."

"Little one! Son!" implored my mother, her ashen face contorted in a horrible expression of suffering. "Animals are eating out my entrails . . . beasts are running through my bones . . ."

"Oh! Oh!" said my father, whose eyes were already rolling back in his head with the vision of death, his skin going dry and black . . .

"Ah! Ah!" said my mother.

And beneath the sheets, her body folded in two and shriveled; her knees almost touched her chin, her mouth rose up twisting to her ears, and her bones cracked.

I ran from one to the other, not knowing what I was doing, losing my head and drunk with vertigo: "Daddy! My poor dad! Mama! My poor mama!"

Crushed by the atrocious sensation of my own powerlessness, I suddenly stopped and fell down on the rug between the two filth-soiled beds, and I covered my ears against the cries, the pleas, and the death-rattles of the two doomed ones that I loved, and I wailed with long laments, long and useless howls, like a dog lost in the night, like a drowning man about to disappear in the black waters of a well.

Oh! What terrible days! Oh, what ghastly nights! How and why was I able to survive the shock and the fear?

When my parents were dead, I was taken by a genuine fit of madness. I didn't want to see those still, decomposing faces anymore; I wanted to escape, far away, very far, to the ends of the world . . . to put the whole universe between those cadavers and myself. I stumbled down the stairs and found myself out in the garden, where I spun around and around like an animal that's been hit in the head. Then I jumped the hedge, crossed the fields, went into town, and started running down the streets, shouting:

"My mom and dad are dead! My mom and dad are dead!"

But the word "dead" no longer summoned any living faces—none that seemed shocked, anyway—to the windows of the houses or the doorsteps. There were dead people in every home. And those who had been spared were trying to escape from the dead, from those who had seen the dead, who had breathed in death. That word, "dead," floated on the silence it could no longer interrupt; it banged on shut windows, at shut-off thresholds, like it was banging on the planks of a funeral bier: the desolation of an orphan. And the coffins passed incessantly through the streets, with no prayers before them, no processions behind. Huge bonfires burned in the squares and courts.

I finally returned to the house . . .

A priest was there, praying by the corpses in the

death chamber. I didn't know him . . . I didn't know where he'd come from. And it seemed to me he was God himself, come down from the sky; his face was that beautiful. In my absence he had cleaned up the beds, washed and dressed the cadavers, put everything in order. He told me, in a very gentle voice: "My poor child! You must not lose courage. You'll need all the courage you have. I'll come back tonight, since you are so alone. I'll spend the night with you, close to them."

But who on earth can boast in the morning that they'll return at night, to anywhere? I learned the next day that the admirable priest, on the night that he was supposed to return, was mown down by the plague.

Oh! If only God were real! If beyond mortal life the gardens of enlightenment could flower, where the good and the just could taste eternal peace!

I was naturally gauche and hesitant. The slightest difficulty had always found me unarmed, not knowing what to do, trembling at the idea of doing anything. Faced with the action that this awful reality demanded, my confusion was extreme. I couldn't make up my mind to accept the smallest responsibility for any of it. For one moment, as I realized I could never manage the details of the funeral, the letters I had to write, the thousand different and painful obligations that such an event demands, I thought of killing myself. I didn't see any other escape from the mess.

And anyway, what would become of me now that I was all alone? How would I live inside that darkness where death had, with one blow, plunged me? I had often dreamed of solitude, had hoped to be free and on my own. And now, what do you know—that solitude and liberty terrified me like a prison. I could no longer even feel the earth under my feet. A great void filled with strange and cruel phantoms surrounded me. It would have been better to die.

Finally, a friend of the family was willing to bail me out. He substituted himself for me with a devotion that was timid at first but soon became admirably heroic. During that horrible plague, the formalities were not fussed over for long. The dead were buried quickly, in big, pre-dug graves, without observing the normal delays. Just the two of us accompanied the two coffins to the church, where short prayers were said, then to the cemetery, where we had to wait two hours for the undertakers to arrive. Then my sisters, who had been ordered to appear by telegram, arrived with their husbands. The house was empty when they went into it; they were pale more from fear than from grief. But they thought that for decency's sake they should moan and cry.

"Oh! My poor father!" said one.

"Ah! My poor mother!" said the other.

My brother-in-law asked suspiciously, "Have they put the legal seals on all of the property?"

And that was all.

My sisters didn't want to see the death chamber, and they kept dragging me away from it. "How did they die? Did they say our names?" . . . They asked no such questions. They settled themselves in the parlour to spend the night on makeshift beds.

Chapter XIII

I had just reached the age of majority when the great misfortune I just recounted crashed down on me. They also pulled my number in the draft that year; but my poor constitution and weak chest made me unfit for service. My family had been hoping the military would take me off their hands; they didn't even get that relief. My poor father used to say:

"If by bad luck his number gets drawn ... well, we'll have to make the best of it."

My poor mother would say:

"It would almost be a good thing ... maybe it would make him less of a ninny!"

My father would add: "Who knows? Maybe he'll make a career out of it ... "

And Mother would say, "Maybe he could become a sergeant!"

These hopes were dashed. I remember my mother's disappointment, the grimace that pursed her lips, when my father came back from the review council saying, "They didn't want him!"

Yes, they didn't even want me for the degrading life of the barracks, the harrowing work of a soldier! I wasn't even good enough for that! And oh, the look they gave me!

As feeble in mind as I was in body, I failed to defend my own interest in the inheritance that came our way so dreadfully and unforeseen. I let my sisters and my brothers-in-law do as they liked, and I didn't protest the exorbitant slices they took.

My sisters tried to justify the theft with arguments from our old household.

"It's right," they explained to me, "that our shares of the inheritance are slightly larger than yours, you must recognise. Or at least it's what Father wanted. You've cost our family a lot of money. We had to pay for you, for years and years of schooling that were very heavy on the budget, very expensive, and cost the rest of us privations of every kind. Then you stayed at home up to this very minute without earning a cent, isn't that true? God knows we've spent enough on your upkeep and instruction! And for nothing! Look, we aren't incriminating you, but you have to understand that instead of being a burden for everyone, you could have been self-sufficient. Look at the other young men around here, the same age as you. If we were to bear the consequences of your laziness or your stupidity, it wouldn't be fair. We didn't cost the family anything—on the contrary, we ran the household, we've worked, we've helped pinch a lot of pennies. So it's very reasonable for us to get it all back now …"

I didn't listen to them. First, I wouldn't have known how to argue such questions; second, my thoughts were elsewhere. I was still too shaken by that horrible drama to attach myself to anything on Earth. I responded mechanically:

"Do what you want . . . I don't care about anything . . ."

My sisters were cautious and orderly women. They wanted to rob me, but they wanted to do it legally and respectably.

So to satisfy the law and put their consciences at ease, they made me sign a renunciation—they antedated it—of all my rights to the estate of my mother, the larger of the two. With this act of humiliation and repentance I confessed to having been a bad son, a spendthrift, whose foul passions and shameful debts nearly ruined his parents. I recognized the shining virtue of my sisters, their disinterest, and their heroism under these sad circumstances, and I begged them to accept the restitution which both my remorse for my past life and justice both commanded me to solemnly make.

I signed that paper; I signed them all. And in so despoiling myself I felt a violent joy. It seemed that ceasing to "possess" unburdened my soul. And in the light of that relief, the love of property appeared to be a crime; and I saw more clearly what I had seen so many times before, in the long months I'd spent at the notary's office: the hideous deformities this passion leaves on people's faces, the feral gleam with which it fills their eyes.

The one thing I wanted was to keep a souvenir of my father. Father had often said, "When I am no more, my gold watch will be for my little boy." But my sisters threw a fit. They claimed that Father had never said such a thing, that just I wanted to rob them; they wouldn't let me take the smallest knickknack. Everything was tossed to the winds of the public auction. They sold everything, down to my mother's dresses, down to some medallions that had been blessed and a small, yellowed holy scapular that still held the scent of the flesh that had given them birth.

When it was all settled, I learned that what remained to me was around eighteen hundred francs a year. It was all the same to me. I hadn't even counted on getting that much. My sisters could have taken everything from me, and it wouldn't have occurred to me to protest. I had only one desire, and that was for them to leave, so I wouldn't have to hear their screeching voices, which had become intolerable to me. I needed to put myself back together, and their presence hampered me, irritated me, and made my thoughts—the few I could still muster after my life was torn apart—dishevel.

The morning of their departure, my older sister said to me:

"So what will become of you now?"

"You got me!" I replied.

Suddenly her voice was no longer so sharp, and her eyes softened. She even tried to affectionately take my hand.

"But you need to think about it. Your future worries me, my poor dear . . . "

Since I said nothing, she kept going:

"I know you can't square everything right this second. But while you wait, where are you going to go?"

"No idea!"

"You aren't being reasonable. Listen—I have an idea. Come with us. I'll house you and feed you; you'll be well cared for, and my husband will give you good advice. He knows lots of people who might be of use to you. And I'll only charge one hundred and twenty-five francs per month."

"No! I don't want to live with you!"

"But why?"

"Because I don't want to! Because I don't want to!"

So, my sister, realizing I wouldn't budge, lifted the mask of hypocrisy and false sentiment she used to hide her soul.

"As you like, dear boy!" she said in a nasty voice. "But just so you know, when you're miserable, it'll be useless for you to come knocking at my door. Go hang, you moron!"

My other sister came at me next, just as sly:

"I understand," she said, "why you didn't accept her proposition . . . But I've never been mean to you. I've always loved you so. Come with me, you'll be pampered, we'll never bother you—you can do what you please—and we'll only charge you a hundred francs per month."

I choked with disgust.

"Go away!" I cried. "Go away! You're ugly! Ugly, hideous! Go away! Oh, how I hate you!"

And as soon as I was alone, in the big empty house that had been sold like everything else, and which I had to leave the next day, an overwhelming fear seized me: "What will I become?" I groaned, collapsing on the parquet.

And I sobbed all night long, yelling over and over: "What will I become? What will I become?"

Chapter XIV

Indeed, what would I become?

Such terrible doubt! A menacing question mark.

I was incapable of taking up anything. My physical weakness, not to mention the prejudices of a ridiculous education, barred me from any manual occupation. My ignorance of everything, which my family had carefully husbanded, disqualified me from what they call, to use the laughable euphemism, "the liberal professions"; and I had an instinctive, invincible disgust for the judiciary, functionary, and administrative vocations, which seemed odious and dishonorable to me, in the sense that they consecrated man's servitude and made his parasitism official. And anyway there was no one around me to push me into anything.

Could I stay out in the country? I had nothing but sad memories there. Everything had become intolerable, even the landscapes I liked best; they were covered over now with a veil of sorrow. And what could you do there anyway? Wallow in laziness, like a larva under its rock? It would've been better to die right then. Because all of these trains of thought eventually arrived at death. It was the necessary, implacable, and almost desirable solution to the unsolvable problem of living.

I vaguely understood that man is made to act, to create; that he possesses a brain in order to dream up ways of life, and muscular energy in order to realize and disseminate them. Although I knew nothing about the mechanism of the world, much less about the mechanism of society, I sensed that all beings, under the threat of decline and death, must obey the supreme law, the law that creates so much movement: work. But paternal authority, as it stuffed me with lies, had killed the kernel of individual conscience that had once lived in me; it had suffocated the spontaneous aspirations that had, for a moment, raised my spirit toward the conquest of things; the scrap of passion that had led me to find desire and beauty in possession—or to put it more truly, in seeking out the mysteries of the earth and the sky.

I tried to rekindle my snuffed enthusiasms. But there was nothing left in me but cold cinders. And I felt the frozen wind of the void on the back of my neck.

To clarify: what I wanted at that point was not to make money. I had enough money to live, or at least to not die of hunger. No desire for lucre entered my soul, I swear it. What I wanted was to act. What I wanted was to use my arms and the blood in my veins, the warm downpours in my brain, for some work—but a work of what? None of my former passions corresponded to any form of human activity. And before the terror of life I was like a sickly child, face to face with a huge boulder that blocks its path, and which it can't budge.

Since then, I've often thought of these things; I've often reflected upon the almost insurmountable difficulty that a young man finds in exercising his faculties in life according to their natural wont. These difficulties are horribly logical. They fit just as well as lies into the universal harmony of malice that we call society. Society is built on a single act: the destruction of the individual. Its institutions, its laws, even its customs—it could never pile them up so many and so strong if it weren't for this criminal task: killing the individual, so it may substitute for what's individual in the man—that is to say, to substitute for his freedom and his spine—an inert, passive, and unproductive lump. And I admire the fact that there were, and are still, beings that are strong enough to have resisted this massive force. What energy! What will! What powerful tenacity, or what inconceivable luck, to be able to survive death, and to show to the dismayed world the miraculous and living face of genius!

At the height of my distress, I found a great joy. I met Lucien one day while I was wandering the fields, masticating these intolerable thoughts.

Lucien was the son of a local butcher. His father had given him a fine education, as mine had done to me. But Lucien was gifted with an uncommon energy. He had escaped the brutality of school with his spirit healthy and his body unbent. When his studies were finished, he notified his father that he wanted to be a painter! When his father refused indignantly, the son fled the paternal estate in the night for Paris. In Paris, he survived endless alternations of hope and poverty. Then father and son were reconciled in the wake of a newspaper article in which Lucien's name was mentioned flatteringly. The good old fellow admired himself in that mirror of vanity that is a printed patronymic, and gave his pardon; so Lucien now came out from time to time to spend a few days out in the country. He worked on his painting there with a singular energy; you would see him in the fields, on the riverbank, stabbing at his easel in every kind of weather and slapping strange colors all over the canvas. To the peace-loving denizens of the boondocks, an artist and a murderer are pretty much the same. They bring with them the same terrors, the fear of an unfamiliar, depraved, and condemned way of life. In a little region like ours, such men were simply outside the law, outside of life. We look away from them, as we do from vagrants in the evening, or devils in their haunted forests at night. My father had forbidden me to fraternize with Lucien— he was a shady good-for-nothing who ate up his parents' money, "and for what? Good God!" This prohibition was painful for me, because Lucien attracted me. He didn't seem like the others; there was a light in his eyes—not at all diabolical—a light like nothing I'd seen in anyone else's eyes. He was a young fellow, just a few years my senior, tall and slender, with a pretty face that was energetic and sweet, lit with a gentle, charming irony and the occasional dash of sadness.

He approached me first:

"Oh, good! You aren't afraid of me, now," he said, holding out his hands.

"Oh, no!" I said. "And I'm so happy to see you. If you only knew. And if you want, I'll see you every day. I'll go with you when you work, I'll carry your gear ... "

The words spilled from me with a real passion. Lucien gave me a look of great kindness that was slightly sad.

"And what are you doing now?" he asked.

"Nothing!" I replied.

And as though a spring had suddenly snapped in my tongue, with an extraordinary flood of words, I told him the entire story of my life. I told him everything that tortured me; the shadows that imprisoned my reason, my desire for the light, and the despair of never, ever reaching it ... all punctuated with violent gestures, my hands clenched so tight that I felt I was clutching a branch stretched out to free me ...

"You're amazing!" Lucien said.

He considered me in silence with his penetrating and melancholy stare, and then he said: "Do you know what's wrong with you? No? Well, I'll tell you: you're an artist. And that's a bad hand to be dealt, you see, because being an artist isn't enough—you have to be a man as well. So there you are."

"Uh ... so, is art beautiful?" I asked.

Lucien replied, "Yes, it's beautiful!"

Then he made a vague gesture: "But everything is beautiful, if you're a feeling person, when you understand things ... well, come along then."

For the two weeks he stayed in the country, I never left his side. The things he said were a marvel to me, but they weren't unfamiliar. It seemed I'd heard them before, and they charmed me like the tune of an old lullaby from my cradle.

When Lucien went back to Paris, I went with him.

Chapter XV

Lucien found a small room for me in the building where he lived. I chose the furniture at random and the books with care, and I made myself at home with confidence and joy. Knowing that Lucien was under the same roof as myself, not far away, made me feel secure. I thought that because of his presence I was less lost, and better protected, in the uncharted waters where I'd just cast myself, even as they rumbled all around my frail person and unquiet soul like a terrible sea. Since he had been able to surmount so many difficulties and prevail over such poverty, he would help me overcome the troubles that were no doubt coming my way. With him on my side, I didn't dread them. As I paced my garret room, contemplating my pauper's decor, it even seemed to me that I had already won the greatest treasure. And I began to read, and read, and read.

Since I'd left the countryside, I really was a different person. Yes, there was something in me that I'd never known was there, something I'd never felt living in me, something I could not have defined, but which lifted me from the earth, made me light, almost weightless really—like in the night, in my dreams, when I traversed the skies with my feet in the void, my head in the stars, my arms stretched out and beating like wings. I was happy. No, I don't exactly mean happy. I was not happy, I was anguished, but with a delicious anguish, the sort of anguish that bites into your heart and fills your chest with the power, delight, or suffering that you feel before a lovers' rendezvous . . .

And I read, I read, I read. I read omnivorously, never able to quench my need; I read avidly, like a wounded man drinking in a burning desert, a wounded man who miraculously finds a spring and plunges his whole head into the cool waters.

One day Lucien said to me:

"Do you want to write? Do you feel something in you that pushes you to do it? . . . Something that makes your hands itch like you're sick, and comes up in your throat like you're about to cry? Is that it? Am I right?"

"I don't know. I couldn't explain, but I'm pretty sure that's what it is . . . "

"Well, listen then, dear boy . . . you read too much. You're gulping things down the wrong tube and digesting them badly, or not digesting them at all. I'm sure that's quite bad for you."

"What should I be doing?"

"You have to live, kid. You'll never find a book—just like I'll never find a painting—that's as valuable as that . . . that thing, that, that . . . well, that . . . how can I express it? . . . Life!"

"Tell me. Advise me. Teach me. I'm still just being born . . . I'm so small, weaker than a child, and it seems like the bones of my skull are still soft to the touch."

"Well, you do understand that writing's not my thing, right? I don't know anything about it. When it's good, I know it's good, and that's about it! I'm looking for something else. I'm looking for ..."

He screwed up his face and traced ideal figures in the air.

"That's what I'm looking for, do you understand? Still, I think that all the arts are a lot alike, whether you're writing, or painting, or sculpting, or putting sounds together ... Yes, I think it's the same sorrow, don't you? Even take a carpenter, for example, a good regular guy who knows nothing about anything. But if he makes a box, or a table, and the proportions are perfect, and the lines are beautiful, well ... do you follow? That's what I think, anyway."

"Please, Lucien, come on!"

"OK, fine. If I were in your place, well! I would go out in the world, walk around. I would roam the streets, along the river, in the parks, everywhere. I would watch people's faces, their backs, and the eyes that passed me by. And then I would ask myself what they meant, and how I could express that. Art, dear boy, isn't just rehashing the work others have done. It's remaking what you have seen with your eyes, felt with your senses, and understood with your mind. Seeing, feeling, and understanding are everything! And then you have to express it too, damn it! But what do you think you can express if you haven't seen anything?—and even what you have seen, you haven't understood!"

"See, feel, understand"—he repeated those three words endlessly. That was all he had to say about aesthetics—in words, anyway. Lucien wasn't eloquent. He actually had a hard time expressing his ideas. When he launched into one of his theories he spat the words out painfully. And once he got a sentence going, it would often trail off into a hand gesture, always accompanied, by way of conclusion, by that trinity of verbs: "To see, to feel, to understand!"

In the mornings I breakfasted hastily at a milk bar on our street, and at night, before dinner, I would go to see Lucien in his workshop. He didn't like people visiting while he was "on a roll," as he put it; and most of the time he locked himself away, wanting solitude and silence. When I arrived at the habitual hour, I would always find him before his canvas, wet with fresh paint; he sat on a low stool, his body bent and folded forward, his chin in his hands, and sucking angrily at a huge pipe. Often he didn't hear me come in. And despite my presence near him, he seemed not to see me; perhaps he didn't see me—and he would stay silent for long moments, grimacing, his eyes full of somber fire, looking at his canvas.

"Oh! It's you!" he would say at last, sounding like he'd been bored before I bothered him.

But then he would get up, cross the workshop with a fevered step, and knock his pipe against the walls to make the ashes fall, crying out from time to time:

"What a pig I am! Dirty bastard! Miserable bastard! And to go on saying, 'Oooh, I feel this!' That I understand it! When I will never, never, be able to capture it! And I'll never, never be able to paint anything, anything!"

Then he'd suddenly grab me roughly by the arm and drag me in front of the canvas and ask: "Look, you! Tell me, what do you think, huh?! Is it vile enough for you?"

His art disturbed me with its audacity and violence. It moved me, terrified me, almost, like the visions of a madman. And I think there was indeed madness infused throughout his works. He would paint trees in the setting sun, their branches twisted and red like flames; or strange night scenes, of wild and vagabond silhouettes on an invisible landscape, under whirling stars and a dancing, pale, and drunken moon that made the sky look like a noisy dancehall. He painted the face of an enigma, mysterious lips, the trajectory of a haggard pair of eyes as they stared out toward who knows what grievous dementia. I obsessed over one particular painting like a vision of death: an immense field of wheat under the sun, a field of wheat with no end in sight, and a tiny reaper with a big scythe, who hurried, and hurried, in vain! Because you knew, you felt how he would never be able to cut all that hay, and that his life would be consumed by that impossible task—and the field, under that sun, would not seem to diminish by a single furrow.

I saw nothing but the incoherence and disequilibrium of his excessive fancies. I was too new to aesthetic emotions to taste their visual beauty and decorative grandeur. I responded, timidly, in a trembling voice:

"That is quite beautiful. But it frightens me a little. I don't know what I'm talking about, of course, but I find it excessive . . . a bit."

Excessive! A word handed down to me by my father, who habitually stamped it on anything that contained a whit of emotion, a thrill of life, a glimmer of thought, or the smallest pulsation of love.

And at that word, Lucien flew into a fit.

"Exaggerated!? Art, you imbecile, is an exaggeration! Exaggeration is a way of feeling, of understanding. It's . . . It's . . . everything, every being, every line . . . everything you see, it all contains a latent value, a beauty you often can't even see! Well then . . . art! Exaggerated! You are an idiot!—you commoner! That's what it is! It's nothing! And I am a brute! Ah, let's go get dinner."

And with a violent gesture, he would turn his canvas back toward the easel—that is, when he didn't bash it in furiously with his fist.

Chapter XVI

After the long days of work, as the evening fell slowly on us, like a theater curtain closing on a bad and useless drama, Lucien often began one of these conversations—or rather, these violent soliloquies, ragged and laced with frightening silences. I observed him as he spoke. He was no longer the same Lucien, that lithe and gentle Lucien, whom I'd met in the country; the clear, dancing lights in his eyes were gone, and he had neither the comely and fine physiognomy, nor that air of youthful serenity, which had lightened my distress with a single stroke and which had attracted me like an asylum of joy, peace, and tranquil power. Power and joy! Oh, poor, poor Lucien!

I remember him vividly, and that image, which after all these years has not left me alone for a single day, still hurts me. The effort it cost to find his words and pronounce them covered his face with deep lines, painfully twisted, like an old man or even a madman. His gaze frightened me in those moments; he stared just like the hallucinatory faces on his canvases; he looked like the tormented, demented skies of his countrysides. I didn't dare say anything. I didn't know what to say. All that I could have said—timid approbation, banal words of comfort—would have been pointless, except to exasperate him further. And I felt that my silence, and the stiffness of my silence, aggravated him even more. He no doubt expected some gesture, an emotion, at least a sign of tacit understanding! But what could I do? A technical philosophical discussion would have turned my mind to less personal reflections, toward general worries. But that would have required me to know how to have such a discussion, and I didn't know anything, I was unable even to rationally digest my reaction to the strange novelty of his works. Nor did I know the phrases people say to comfort and reassure each other. I searched for them hopelessly in my sad and frightened heart. I did not find them.

And then there was the dread that was growing in me every day; a dread that shook me like a gust of wind shakes a flimsy stalk, a pitiful little weed with no one to look after it. Was Art really such torture, such a hell? My dreams were still vague, and in them I had imagined it as such a great comfort; an ideal, impossible, infinite paradise where men created nothing but happiness. So was I, too, going to spend my life gasping for air, with my face twisted and my eyes pulsing with the pale light of insanity? The thought sent a chill down my spine. I wouldn't have stayed there—I would have run far away—every time I saw Lucien preyed upon by these crises; I wanted to flee, to go back to the country, where you never see any human faces that aren't thoughtless, any eyes that aren't dull, just faces and eyes like flat waters. Except I didn't dare run. I was fixed there despite myself, tied by some mysterious and horrible pleasure to the torture of being there. The growing shadows in that atelier seemed more tragic by the minute. Objects reared up in a sinister fashion, bloating to the surreal proportions of a nightmare; the painted faces came to a terrifying life—leaning over me with a supernatural stare—their mouths like vulvas, torn by a cruel snicker. The easels began to look like crucifixes, dangling their atrocious victims. Total fear seized me and I cried out:

"Lucien! Lucien! Please! Let's get out of here!"

Out in the street, I calmed down a bit, and little by little Lucien did as well. His discouragement took on a less gloomy form; his hopes for tomorrow's labors would spark a new little glimmer of confidence, and I watched with joy as his body relaxed, erasing the lines in his face and untwisting his mouth. For me, the noise of the street, the flow of the city, the bright shops, and the jostling of passers-by served to chase the phantoms from my brain. Lucien slipped his arm into mine, and walking along, he said in a softer voice:

"Painting! Kid, you can't imagine how hard it is—it might even be impossible! I've often suspected the whole racket could be nothing but a hoax, like everything else. Who knows? But anyway, there are two problems in painting. First you have to show the essence of the thing you're painting—the design, if you like. And then you have your technique. Ah, the technique! Like . . . for example, say you're in a garden, right? Now, say that in this garden, there are flowers, groups of flowers, of different colors that all clash with each other. Theoretically, you'd imagine that it would be jarring. It would have to be. But no, not at all! In nature, it's always beautiful. Nature doesn't give a damn about theories! I'll tell you why. Nature, or light, if you prefer, performs a . . . how shall I put it . . . chemical reaction? No, not chemical . . . eh, it doesn't matter. Anyway, on her own, without its being visible to the eye, she uses imperceptible juxtapositions of nuances to guide the change from one hue to another. It's this invisible passage that the painter must see and reproduce on the canvas to give the approximation of natural harmony that he needs. You can only do it by graduating the shades . . . that's it. Christ! You know, in school, they don't even suspect this . . ."

Then, brusquely, he cut himself off, and stuck me with his elbow, saying:

"But what a face you made earlier! And why'd you want to leave? Were you ill?"

I confessed to the fear that had seized me, and I described to him my strange visions in the workshop. Lucien was exultant:

"Well, there you go! That's art, little one. That's art! Visions? But you are a child; you've discovered the spirit of the things in the workshop, no more, no less. An easel that looks like a cross, like a gallows? Bravo! That's it! That's its essence! You have given that object, which is nothing, which has no real existence, the form of the terrors in your soul! Tomorrow, perhaps, you'll see it differently, you'll see it as . . . as a cathedral . . . as a great sunflower. You really have to get this truth through your head: a landscape, a face, any object—they don't exist in themselves. They only exist in you. You imagine that there are trees, plains, rivers, seas. That is a mistake, my good fellow. None of that exists, in the end anyway. All of that is in you, and that's much tougher, it seems to me. A landscape is a state of your spirit, like anger, like love, like despair. And the proof is that if you paint the same place when you're happy and then on another day when you're sad, it doesn't look the same at all. 'Nature this, nature that.' By God! I do believe her! She is admirable . . . admirable in this respect—mark my words—in that she doesn't exist, that she's nothing but an idealized, multifarious trick of your mind—an emotion inside of your soul! 'Ooh, a tree, a tree!' So what, there's a tree! What does it prove? Your naturalist painters make me laugh, they don't know what nature is. They think a tree is a tree, and always the same tree! What idiots! One little tree is thirty-six thousand different things! It's an animal sometimes, it's, it's . . . how should I know? It's all that you see, all that you feel, all that you understand! I may say it very badly, but I'm telling you the truth all the same!"

And he shook my arm roughly, like a branch, and kept saying:

"It's obvious, look! Look, you can't ignore it!"

These words, in which I found so many incoherencies and contradictions, did not reassure me. But they dissipated quickly into the air, and only a discordant sound stayed with me, like a fountain engineer's horn losing itself in the noise of the city.

We arrived thus, with him drunk on his own words and me deafened from hearing them, to the pension where we usually dined. It was a sad, modest little boarding house, frequented by government workers and faceless bourgeois men without families. Lucien had chosen it for exactly these qualities, as "a change of scenery," as he called it. As much as he could, he avoided the artsy milk bars and literary cafés. It was sort of an intellectual haven, a truce with the preoccupations "that racked his head and soured his stomach." And he chattered with the regulars gaily about stupid things: politics, food, and women.

"They're morons!" he said to me the first evening. "But tragic, as you'll see. I don't think there's anything as awful as a fat, bald bourgeois! All the ferocity of humanity is in him, my boy. It's like a picture! Delacroix made a sentimental and romantic little ladies' man out of Hamlet. A face like a lovestruck hairdresser, skinny with big sunken eyes . . .

"But that's stupid! Think of Shakespeare's Hamlet, how he must look in the morning. A fat man with a gut, smothered in pale flab and weighed down with beer: He's a Dane, after all. And do you see those enigmatic, haggard eyes, the eyes of a mournful humbug—do you see them, trapped behind their lids? In the washed-out fat face, behind the dishwater hair? Brrr! But, there you are. For all his genius, Delacroix lived in stupid times— stupid! And as for Victor Hugo! What a bore! What did he see? What did he understand? I'd rather listen to the wind in the pines and the organs in the churches. At least they don't make speeches, and they have something to say . . . what a loser!"

We stayed there for two hours. Lucien laughed at the bourgeois' puns and pinched the maid's thighs whenever she passed by. His vulgar manners upset me. But I still preferred to see him this way.

"Ah! Monsieur Lucien!" the maid simpered. "Knock it off already!"

And Lucien, with a rude, childish gesture, replied:

"I'm just kidding, my little kitten. You know me. I only sleep with my paintings. That's enough for someone like me."

Chapter XVII

When we left the boarding house we would take long detours across Paris toward home. More than anything, Lucien loved to wander in the evening along the darkened quays. The nocturnal landscapes affected him strangely. He walked through the night like a preacher in his chapel, at a slow pace, attentive and respectful. All of his senses awoke and vibrated; his spirit stretched out toward ecstasy. He genuinely felt the night; he touched it, he drank it down like wine from a chalice.

And from time to time, to express his enthusiasm he would say: "Ah! Hell!"

Then, between silences:

"Look at these tints! How do you render those, do you have any idea? And color isn't the whole story ... There's the odor, yes, the scent of the night! Have you smelled the night? Do you feel it?"

And he sucked in the air, with a great noise from his nostrils.

"It smells ... ? Huh, that's funny. It's smells like a cat that's been sleeping in the manger."

And he swept his hands through the air, as if he were petting an animal, with slow caressing gestures.

"And it's soft like a pelt! Ah, hell!"

After that, he'd spend a quarter of an hour in silence, not even responding to the questions I asked him, absently making gesticulations whose meaning escaped me.

One day, I recall, he was resting his elbow on the railing of a bridge. I copied him. And we stayed that way for a long time, without moving, without speaking. Beneath us, the black river rolled its waters, all sequined with dots of light, the watered-silk reflections rippling like a ball gown; the buildings along the river drew shadowy perspective lines with their parallel masses, touched with trembling spots of light; in the distance, the sparkling arcs of the bridges reflected their lights in the waves, snaking in scattered and fluctuating zig-zags, or better yet plunging in incandescent colonnades, into the infinite depths, into copper-colored skies turned upside-down. Some sharp silhouettes appeared here and there, on backdrops of pale firmament; more vague silhouettes, shadows upon shadows, glided soundlessly on the river.

"It's beautiful, isn't it?" Lucien asked me.

"Yeah, it's beautiful," I replied, mechanically and without conviction, because when I was in Lucien's presence, I could no longer feel a personal sensation. He absorbed me to the point where nothing outside of him existed anymore for me. He had so derailed my spirit that I no longer dared pursue an idea, nor enjoy a spectacle, without fearing that it wasn't "art." Most of all, I dreaded his constant demands that I explain why I found some particular thing beautiful.

He repeated his question.

"So, you find it beautiful?"

"Yeah, yeah, sure!"

"All right, kid . . . do you know what I'm thinking?"

"No, Lucien . . . "

"Well, kid, I think it's killing us . . . "

As accustomed as I was to my friend's bitter words, I lifted my head toward him, disturbed and confused.

"What's killing us?" I said. "What are you saying?"

"I'm saying the city!" Lucien declared, making a gesture so large it embraced all of Paris.

The Seine sang gently around the pillars of the bridge; the far-off call of a tramway horn faded and died between the parapets.

"Why do you say that, Lucien?"

"Because I hope Paris burns! Because all cities should be burned to the ground!"

"Why do you say that, Lucien?!" I insisted.

"Because I'm not happy! Are you happy? And do you think they're happy—the two million creatures who live here, who're going God only knows where, and who want God knows what? And there won't be any beautiful art—that is to say a beautiful life, because it's all the same—until Paris is no more."

He pulled himself together and turned his back on the river, and, sitting down on the stones, he put his hands on my shoulder . . .

"Everything that's strong, everything that's good, Paris entices and devours. Paris takes the best of us and turns us into madmen or losers. I think I'm going insane here, myself. Paris is eating my brains out, eating my heart, breaking my arms. We won't be happy till there's nothing left but fields, plains, forests . . . "

Lucien was incapable of following a line of reasoning for very long. He jumped from one idea to another without transition, so fast that it made made his conversation hard to understand. Or rather, the transitions were ellipses in which the links between the ideas were hidden from me. He suddenly asked: "Have I shown you my study, The Dunghill?"

"No!"

"What, I haven't shown it to you? It's of nothing. It's simply an autumn field at harvest time, and in the middle, there is this huge pile of refuse. Well, my boy, when I painted that . . . I remember . . . Ah! Son of a bitch! Have you ever really looked at a dunghill? It's got a certain mystery! Imagine . . . a ton of filth, at first blush, strewn with whatever . . . but then, if you look closer, see how the mass begins to move, to expand, to rise, groan, come to life . . . and with how many lives? Forms appear, the forms of flowers, of beings, breaking their embryonic shells. It's a wonderful frenzy of germination, an enchantment of flora, of fauna, headsful of hair, an explosion of splendid life! I tried to render that, to get the feeling, but screw it! I need, do you see, I need to go see a dunghill again, some dirt, some clumps of earth, eh? I'm going to take off tomorrow, for a month, maybe two. I'm going, I don't know where . . . maybe I'll go really far away . . . "

"Can I come with you, Lucien?" I begged.

"No, no I have to be alone. When I'm like this, I shouldn't talk. You'll work while I'm gone."

We went back home without a word. I followed Lucien up to his workshop, where he packed a little suitcase with his case of canvases and colors. He interrupted his ministrations several times to tell me:

"And you'll see! Paris will fall. When people have enough of coming in from their forests, their mountains, their plains, just to crack their heads on its stones, Paris will burn, I tell you! There'll be nothing left of it but the stink. A great poet once said: 'The spot where a theater used to be always smells like a rat that died under the floor . . . ' If you're talking about a city, let's say it smellls like a bourgeois dead in his wine cellar. And that'll be it. All right, little one, go to bed, kiss me, and I will see you later."

Indeed, Lucien left the next day. He was as happy as a bird at dawn, singing his lungs out in a rowan tree.

Chapter XVIII

I was so accustomed to living with Lucien, to acting and thinking through him, that when I was alone again and deprived of my guide, it seemed to me I was once more lost in a desert; and without Lucien, Paris was just as sad and empty to me as that big house back home had been after the death of my parents. Despite my horror of solitude, I did not want to go eat my meals at our familiar spots, due to my natural timidity, but also out of disgust at the crude jokes that ornamented the conversation of the vulgar patrons, who, competing for attention in the presence of an artist, were inspired to creepy laughter and annoying familiarities.

Nor, for anything in the world, would I have consented to spend my evenings in the café Lucien had taken me to several times, where he'd introduced me to some young artists and writers, friends of his who met there every day. Amongst these rising and intimidating celebrities I had yet to make a friend. Afraid to speak, clumsy, and ill-versed in the transcendental questions that were being resolved around me, I was very well aware that, in this milieu of battling theories and stormy aesthetics, I was just a rather ridiculous interloper, and that I counted for less than the sticky bench I was crammed onto, or an empty beer glass being swept across the table by the grand gesture of a poet, spokesman for the Ideal.

While Lucien was gone I resolved to see no one, and to never go out, except in the evening, when habit drew me to the favored haunts of our nocturnal promenades. Lucien had entrusted his studio keys to me. It was there, in that room, so filled with him that it groaned at the seams with his presence, that I spent my days. In that chamber of his daily torture, I tried ardently to get down to work. When Lucien returned, I wanted to show him something of myself. But the work was terribly painful to me, because my spirit was empty of myself, and it was Lucien that I found at the bottom of the things I was trying to describe, of the ideas I tried to express—an anaemic Lucien, winded and impotent. And my mind was so unhinged from the substitution of another personality for my own that I could no longer look at the most banal object in tranquility. I couldn't look at a broom, or a pen-stand, for example, without managing to create an entire world of nightmares from it, to make frightening and supernatural analogies with it—without hearing an interior voice, a voice that was my voice and Lucien's strangely mixed together, crying to me: "That's it . . . More . . . Seek even more mystery and more terror! That's spirit. That is art!" My imagination spent itself on these games; my brain, working endlessly over impossible combinations of forms, bruised itself. And after my vain battles with these phantoms, with my limbs raddled and a torpid head, I would sink into deathlike prostrations. Death was in me and all around me, like a pale, immense abyss, like a great motionless sky, crossed from time to time by flocks of chimerical birds, flights of bewildered animals, transfigurations of my deranged thoughts.

Instead of taking a reinvigorating plunge into the bath of life that would renew me—instead of reclaiming my memories of innocence, the gentle ironies of my childhood, the emotions of the old countryside, simple and tranquil—I sank, every day, every hour, deeper into that evil fever. When night fell, I would tear myself from my shadowy hole like a bat and prowl the quays, the bridges, anywhere Lucien and I had spent hours together in dreary reverie; I went again to see the troubled obscurity, to try to find, in the shuddering of the dark, lamp-spangled waters, the painful, mad laments that Lucien had tossed into them. I came home late, broken down, my legs weak, my throat clutched with an unspeakable anguish, and I fell into a painful sleep, the sleep of a sick man devoured by fever.

And it was then that for the first time my heart was awakened to love.

Poor little Julia! Frail and slow, and very fair haired, with the pale skin of a hothouse flower. Oh! Her hands were so white. And her look, her look was so sweet, the gaze of a sick girl who searches people's eyes for the fatal secret their lips won't betray! A look so sad and artless, and yet alluring, and full of love! How I loved her, the first time that gaze rested upon me, like a bird perching on a dead branch!

Julia was our concierge's daughter. Up to this point she'd been out working for a seamstress; but she'd become too weak and sick, no one knew why. Her parents had taken her back in. All day long, it was her job to look after the conciergerie, a little lodge where they lived and looked after the building. The mother did house cleaning; the father was an office boy in a banking firm. Accommodating, lovely, always smiling, she acknowledged everyone who came by, and everyone slowed down a bit, happy to look at her. It seemed that her mere presence had cleared away the smell of old grease that usually filled the narrow quarters, and replaced it with the perfume of a young fresh flower. Every time I came in or out, I went through that conciergerie, where I nearly always found her alone, and I'd ask were any letters for me, or for Lucien. And after she replied, I would stay there, standing before her, not saying anything more, a bit stunned by my own audacity and annoyed by my silence. She said no more either. She would begin to arrange little knick-knacks, poor little trinkets, on a shelf, or to feather-dust the ranks of chromolithographs that decorated the walls. And I felt my heart melt into unknown delights, just watching the curls quiver on the back of Julia's ivory neck.

"All right, I'll see you later, Mademoiselle Julia."

"Till later, Monsieur!"

"And if we get any letters, don't send them up. I'll get them."

"Very well, Monsieur."

"All right, till later, Mademoiselle Julia."

"I'll see you later, Monsieur!"

And it seemed to me that her smile held a slight and charming irony, and a comprehension of everything I didn't say aloud; it was all there in the awkwardness of my gestures, in the timidity of my eyes.

One day she said to me:

"Oh! Monsieur, I'd be so happy if you would lend me some books."

My heart pounded violently. Those words were like a kiss. I stammered:

"I don't have any books. But I'll get some. Mademoiselle Julia, what books would you like me to give you?"

I had regained a bit of my equilibrium.

"Oh, I don't know . . . beautiful books that make you cry!" she said.

"You mean books about love, do you?"

Just saying that word, "love," made my face turn red.

An expression of joy lit Julia's whole face. "Oh! Yes! Books about love! Books like they lent me at the shop!"

My blood ran hotter through my veins; my muscles felt stronger, ready for a virile embrace.

"I'll go find you some books!" I said, my voice resolute and brave.

I left like a hero going off to conquer a new world.

When I returned, loaded with volumes, the mother was in the lodge; I didn't dare go in, and I went back up to Lucien's workshop.

That day I didn't have to wrestle with phantoms. Every form was divine, every color radiant. It was like an explosion of flowers within me, magnificent and pure; it was like a wave of perfumes washing over me.

And I never stopped repeating to myself Julia's phrase, the phrase that sounded to me like a revelation of love:

"Beautiful books that make you cry! . . . "

Chapter XIX

My enthusiasm lasted several days. During this flush of exaltation, I didn't think for an instant to milk it for literary artifice, nor did I seek the "artistic quality" of the new and violent sensations that I felt in my soul. I rejoiced in them un-intellectually and totally, like a bull savors the spring grass where it buries its jowls. Even the image of Lucien itself dissipated; and the canvases in the workshop, so full of despair, were covered with a veil of hope.

In the cabal of the little café, I had heard the young poets celebrate the love of famous courtesans and princesses. They talked of nothing but gilt cloth, folds of brocade, gems of green chrysoprase; they evoked only the haughty and voluptuous faces framed by royal décor and stained glass that irradiate their own glorious flesh. For them, love was just a sumptuous landscape, with lakes and gondolas, armor, castle towers, and marble staircases rustled over by the gliding trains of gowns. My happiness, on the other hand, grew from the humble and poor state of my beloved. She was pretty—or so she seemed to me. But I would have preferred her to be ugly, so I'd love her all the more.

My days passed by almost entirely within her somber and ill-kempt lodge, which my overexcited imagination transformed into an incomparable palace. When tenants, visitors or merchants came to interrupt our ecstasies, I would hide, my heart pounding, in the narrow adjoining room that served as a kitchen. There, on a greasy little cast-iron stove, the family's broth was always boiling; on a board, on a cracked plate, a piece of spleen was being bled, and black rags hung everywhere. I didn't see these vulgar details, which would've disconcerted the young poets; Julia's presence ennobled all these things, despite their lowly indiscretion, and that sordid kitchen was more mysterious to me than a chapel. From that chapel, where the stubborn smells of grease stood in for incense, I watched Julia as she served the visitors; her blonde locks, the coquettish smiles on her lips, the charming inclination of her long waist, her fingers playing with the doorknob, filled me with unspeakable dreams and an unearthly love. Oh! How I loved her sad, tattered taffeta bustier and the faded fringes that adorned it; and her hunched neck—how touching!—despite the er . . . how to put it delicately—ring of dirt—poor Julia—that darkened it above her collar! She wasn't very well-groomed; no. But she was so sweet, so good, so tender!

What bothered me was that when I was near her, I didn't know what to say. My heart was full of inexpressible things; there were no words to describe what I felt. Also, most of the time, we remained silent; but how eloquent that silence was, aided by the mute and ardent language of our gazes! It was only in the garret, alone, that I regained my self-possession and the liberty of my declamatory faculties. I spoke to the absent Julia with an extraordinary abundance of passionate phrases; I crawled on my knees, wrapped my arms around her waist, and through my tearful supplications, my intoxicated words and bold gestures, we came to mix our kisses and rise, the two of us, toward marvellous and unknown heavens! From these play-acts of love, where I played both roles, I would always come back to earth a bit sad and disgusted. After the exaltation there came a moment of terrible depression, when the idol appeared to me stripped of its ideal, when I saw vividly the ridiculousness of my solitary pantomime.

"If Lucien had seen me!" I would say to myself. "If he knew I spent my days in that place!"

And the shame would rise to my face, in red and burning waves.

But it was enough for me to go downstairs, to see Julia behind the curtains of the conciergerie, to win back my enthusiasm and float away again into the great blue dream.

Our conversations—broken by long silences—relied almost entirely on the novels I'd given to Julia. Julia told me about all the little twists of these dramas, so unfamiliar to me. She lent such a disjointed passion to these stories, such paucity of mind, such a vulgar sentimentalism that, in any other circumstance, I'd have found it supremely comical, irresistibly ridiculous. But I'd never have dreamt of laughing at her new episodes of the "Roman chez la portiere." On the contrary, my emotions were, naturally, Julia's. Our pulses raced together, we felt the same surges of admiration, the same indignation, the same immense pity. I still remember one adulterous countess who drew plenty of tears from us.

One afternoon, Julia was giving me an anguished account of a riveting scene. It was about the countess and her lover. As the scene was passionate and explicit, Julia was using rather embarrassed circumlocutions ... when she came to the definitive moment, she hunched up on her chair, spread her hands on her dress and was suddenly quiet.

"So then, Julia ... why don't you go on?" I asked.

"Because ... I can't say those sorts of things ... you wouldn't like me any more."

"Oh! Julia! No, go on! How could I not like you anymore? That's crazy!"

"But it's true, it's true!"

"Julia! My little Julia! Please ... Julia ... go on."

"No! No!"

Her mouth was open, her lips trembling ... it looked as though her dilated nostrils were drinking in some strange perfume, and her eyes were filled with small, bright flames. I took her hand and clenched it; "Julia!" I repeated, in a deep, grave voice.

She didn't reply. But her hand clutched at mine.

"Julia!" I cried hoarsely.

And as though I had been struck by a cruel intoxication, everything spun and teetered around me. Mindlessly, I felt my hand drop hers and wander over her flesh, violating her. Julia cried out, and defending herself, pushing me away, she then covered her face with her hands.

"Oh! Oh! Oh!" she said.

I sat there stupefied by my caddishness. I turned my head away and my arms fell to my sides, inert. But I went on stuttering: "Julia . . . I've hurt you . . . "

"Oh! Oh! Oh!" she was still saying.

"Julia! Please pardon me!"

"Oh! Oh!" she repeated still.

I begged her:

"Julia! Julia! I'm not a bad man! Don't think about it anymore! I'll never, never talk to you about that again! It's over! I swear to you that it's over! Please forgive me—I went mad!—but it's finished!"

Then I dared to look at her, timidly, fearfully . . .

Her face was still hidden in her hands, her neck bent, that innocent throat where her blonde locks played, those virginal blonde curls, hanging there like a violent reproach to my brutality! And then my heart learned all the delicious ecstasies, all the delicacies of repentance . . .

"Give me your hand, Miss Julia," I solemnly pronounced. "You have nothing more to fear from me."

"Is that really true?" she said.

"I swear!"

"That was so low, what you did! Here at my mother's house! And all the people who could have walked in . . . "

She uncovered her face. Her eyes, a bit red, no longer showed shame, nor horror, nor astonishment. I was even a bit disappointed when she gave me a little ironic look. Yet she gave me her hand, which I held for a few seconds in mine.

"Goodbye, Miss Julia."

"Goodbye, Monsieur."

And I went back up to the workshop, my mind clouded; I no longer knew what I was feeling.

<u>Chapter XX</u>

In the midst of these new preoccupations, I received the following letter from Lucien:

Ecluses de Porte-Joie.

As soon as you get this letter, dear boy, pack up all the paint tubes and white canvasses that are left in my workshop. Address the package to me at the Café de la Marine, Ecluses de Porte-Joie. A pretty name, eh?— and a reassuring one! An admirable place, where one must be happy, if the name doesn't lie, the way that one's enthusiasm does. "The Door to Joy!" That's the place where I'm staying, for the moment; there I will stay another month, maybe longer, perhaps forever, because it's crammed my head with considerable projects, and I await some vertiginous events which will completely flummox you, should they come about. I can't say any more about it right now. Be content to dream on what I don't say. Above all, don't imagine there's a woman involved in this escapade. You know what I think about that subject. Women—Bah! Too un-aesthetic!

You'll find two hundred-franc bills pinned to this letter. With this money, pay off my lease, the concierge, and the paint dealer, who will give you my bill around the 15th. It'll be eighty-three francs. With the rest, go wild. I figure you'll have about 70 centimes, heh heh ... That's it for the business end.

Now for something else.

Since I left you, I've been hiking a lot, and I've stumbled upon outlandish motifs, striking landscapes, one after another ... Christ! Imagine you're in a narrow valley, between gentle slopes, half pink chalk, half pines, undulating marvelously where the Seine is wide. In its milky waters, under the sweet sky, are sprinkled numerous little islands covered with poplars. From a distance, halfway up the hill, they look like vagabond cathedrals, like gigantic naval fleets—or rather like the Atlantides, victorious after ages spent buried in the sea, resurging from the wrack-blackend depths into the brilliant light of life. All very well, but go try to capture the majesty of that in art!

I've painted a lot as well, and I haven't produced anything but mountains of crap. I've wrecked almost all of my canvases in a rage, except for two sketches that aren't too bad, and which will help me later on with a great scene I'm dreaming of. Or at least I like to console myself with this illusion. But how often I've dreamed the same way of things that will never be realized!

About those two sketches: so, imagine me, coming home with all my gear. To go up to my room, I have to cross the great room of the café. A bourgeois was sitting there. The bourgeois are rare in these parts. There's too much air, too much wind, too much sky for them, they couldn't live with all this light and beauty. It was a bourgeois from a nearby town. He had yellow boots decked with spurs, a tie, and perhaps a horse tied up in the courtyard. But I didn't see the horse. Innocently, with no aggressive intention, I leaned my canvasses against a chair, face up, as I was tired of carrying them. At first, the bourgeois didn't see them. He was quite occupied in demanding, in authoritative terms, a vermouth that they were slow in serving him. And the intrusion of a suspicious character, poorly dressed and paint-smeared as I was, sure wasn't going to calm him down. At the same time that he was cursing out the servant girl, he eyeballed me with disdain. All of a sudden he noticed my sketches leaning on the chair, with their great slashes of vermilion, their turbulent yellow swirls. And it was like someone had kicked him in the behind. In a flurry of rapid, expressive, and simultaneous movements, watch the unhappy bourgeois as slouches his shoulders forward, throwing out his spine behind; he pinched his buttocks and balled his fists up on them, twisted his mouth, and bugged out his eyes in the most horrible grimace a monkey could ever invent. The maid arrived with his vermouth at that moment of pathos; he slammed the drink, choked on it, snorted, sneezed, and left, clenching his derriere as he protected it from more imaginary boots with the double cuirass of his hands. For a few minutes, I congratulated myself upon the thundering sincerity of his clearly involuntary, yet poignantly critical, fit. But later, alone in my room, face to face with these canvases, I said to myself that the bourgeois, after all, was correct, and my painting was rotten.

I feel, dear boy, more and more disgusted with myself. The more deeply I penetrate nature, into the inexpressible and supernatural mystery that is the world, the more I feel how weak and powerless I am before such beauty. We can perhaps picture nature with the mind, vaguely—but to express it with the gauche, gross, untrue tool that is the human hand—I believe it's beyond the power of man. And so why try? What does it matter to miserable humanity if I paint my poplars red, yellow, blue, or green?—if I tranquilly dot my oranges and violets around to simulate the waters of a river or the imponderable ether of a sky, while in real life, at every step, we collide with monstrous iniquities and unacceptable sorrows? Will I destroy those with my paintbrush, will I save anybody with my palette knife?! Yes, I'm suffering cruelly, from the more and more firm notion that art might be nothing but a con, an imbecilic mystification, and something even worse: a cowardly, hypocritical desertion of social duty!

In the country, in the silent little villages, where man is more sparse and less hidden than in the anonymous, shrieking cities, he sees better what weighs on him, what overshadows him; he realizes the terrifying servitude to which he's condemned, the eternal indenture . . .

Here's an example. The other day, I met a little old man who was bemoaning his lot. And listen to what he told me. One morning he was fixing the wall of his cottage on the side of the road. A government surveyor came by and gave him a ticket. It seems—can you believe this?—that you don't have the right to replace a stone that's fallen from your own wall without first getting a permit from the prefect. The poor old guy had to stop work, and he'll have to pay a hundred-franc fine for the crime of sticking two shovels of mortar to his ruined wall! But how beautiful that old peasant was, standing behind his wall telling me of his miseries! The faded blue of his shirt was the corner of an April sky!

And it's always so. Man doesn't have the right to move toward joy, to grasp happiness, to think, to imagine, to create, even to feel. It's appalling, if you think about it . . . as soon as a man wakes to consciousness, as soon as he realizes he has legs and can walk, the State comes in and breaks his legs with a billyclub. But a man has arms as well; if he can no longer walk, he can grab something. So the State comes back and breaks his arms with a stick. So he's flat on the ground. But he has a brain, which makes him always a contender, because he can think, he can dream; there the idea of human redemption is seeded and flowers, there blooms the sublime flower of rebellion. So the state comes back a third time and smashes his skull with a mallet, and says to him, "There, now you're a good citizen."

Yes! I like poor people, I love them with a tenderness as immense as human sorrow. I love them, not just because their bodies and accents are lovely, but because all of society's infamy shines in the protuberances of their bones, the calluses of their hands, and I want . . . oh! I don't know what I want . . . but I feel there's something more beautiful, maybe greater than art . . . love!

Well, there you have it! But none of that will keep me from returning to my work with a vengeance!

    Love,
      Lucien

P.S. As soon the event occurs, I'll write to you. Don't forget the rent, the concierge, and the paint seller. You know how I hate being sued. I'm counting on you.

This letter left me very sad. My heart was heavy when I finished it. Because there was not a word for me, not a word of tender interest, not even a glimmer of curiosity about my life. I felt something like jealousy gnawing at my heart, and for a minute, it seemed to me that I no longer loved Lucien.

Chapter XXI

The malaise, or rather the sort of disappointment, that Lucien's letter caused me lasted several days. It made me suffer greatly, and the ruminations that it foisted on me disturbed my feelings of friendship—and, even more, troubled the more reasonable and down-to-earth conceptions of art and life that I held, without admitting it to myself, at the core of my being. Under the veneer of refined sensibility, which I had long believed made me different from my parents, I found the same intellectual inferiority that I'd been born to, the same hereditary tics, the same fearful little bourgeois soul, unfit for grand exaltations of thought. I understood better how Lucien with his furious vision of things was dangerous to me, and how he assaulted my ordinary, tranquil feelings. He was taking me with him down a terrible path which had no end but despair, because he was chasing, and obliging me to chase, unconscionable mirages in whose existence he wasn't even sure he believed. I didn't want to seek any deeper into the matter. Too many questions, terrifying questions, tied into it; and I'd already decided to push away all the troubling preoccupations, everything that could darken the surface calm of my life with a menacing cloud.

One morning, when I felt freer than usual from the diabolical influences that turned my soul into the shadow of Lucien's, I decided to take pleasure in my own self, to enjoy life as I perceived it. I resolved to spend the entire day strolling along the streets, looking at beings and objects, not through Lucien's troubled eyes, but with my own eyes, insofar as they belonged to me anymore.

I descended the five floors from my room, alert, almost gay, my muscles stimulated as though by an electric current. Walking past the conciergerie at a calculated slow pace I saw Julia sitting with her head bent over a book. Above her, a cineraria of an unbearable blue was wilting in a pot, and in another pot on the hearth, between two photographs, were two crossed peacock feathers, nearly bald, their greenish eyespots filmed with dust. In this setting Julia looked very sallow to me, her face withered, with a too-long neck that gave her the attitude and expression of a ridiculous bird. And how her bodice of thin, faded, patched, threadbare stuff betrayed her hideous poverty! It drowned all thoughts of delicious softness. At the sound of my tread, she lifted to me her sad forehead, where two sad locks of wan, sick-looking hair hung disheveled. I greeted her with a distant and guarded air; I was in no mood that morning to pity an anemic concierge. On the contrary, it wouldn't have displeased me to cruelly mock her skinniness, the empty pockets that her blouse left at the top of her corset, or the hard angularity of her throat—all those physical imperfections which I, in that state of low vengeance and vile spite, took an odious pleasure in discovering and detailing, like a lover coming to his senses after the act of possession. No doubt, she saw everything awful that was crawling in my soul, and she amplified her gaze as if to envelop me head to foot in a halo of tenderness. Then she rose from her chair, closed her book, opened the door, and with a melancholy smile, gave me a sweet hello, a gentle and tender hello, to which I felt compelled to reply with a cold grunt. She sighed:

"Ah! How mean you seem today!"

With great dignity I replied, "I'm not mean, Mademoiselle. I'm in a hurry."

"So, you won't come in just for a minute?" She hunched back to let me come in.

"No, really, Mademoiselle, I can't come in . . . I'm really in a hurry."

But as I was saying I wouldn't come in, I had pushed the door open further and entered the lodge.

"Oh, how nice!," Julia simpered. "I was afraid you were angry."

"And why would I be angry? I'm not angry . . . I'm in a hurry. Those are two different things, if you ask me."

"All right then, sit down for a little bit!" As she spoke she giggled a little, showing her slightly rotted teeth, coated here and there with blackish tartar.

As always, the kitchen was open, with the family's broth simmering on the stove and the cat's food being bled on the board. The smell of onions swirled in the air; at the end of the room was the bed, magisterially adorned with a throw of fake guipure lace that outlined the pillow with its transparent pinkness and flowed over the thick, checkered open-work quilt.

Julia said, "Ah! Why are you so cruel? And why are you so handsome today? More handsome than usual . . . "

I sat down near her, on a low chair, in a dark corner, and all my stiffness and arrogance disappeared. I sighed as I pressed my friend's hand, and my heart filled with repentance and tender pity.

"Ah! Julia! . . . Julia!"

I squeezed her hand, and passed our two joined hands over her and over myself. Julia didn't defend herself. She only said, "Be careful . . . you have to be wise . . . if you aren't, I'll think that you don't love me."

To a more audacious and targeted caress, she responded, "No! No! Not that. Don't ask me for that . . . "

And then, in a softer voice, as her flesh began to quiver: "Think about it: if someone came by! For you, since you're a man, it doesn't mean anything! But me? Look, if something bad happened, what would become of me? Be wise, please, I don't want to . . . "

Protesting all the while, she gave herself up to the most delicate investigations of her person, even mixing her caresses with mine, caresses more expert than my own. And suddenly her head was writhing on my chest.

"You're maddening me . . . you drive me crazy!" she cried.

Her eyes were avid, and so were her lips, and so was the tone of her breathless voice that her approaching passion rendered hoarse, torn up by the blunt resonance of animality. Soon she was reduced to mewing, the plaintive little wail of a child; several times, as her body loosened and her mind melted, she cried, "Mama! Mama!"

I tasted an incomplete joy, which left me deeply saddened and a little bit bewildered.

As for Julia, she hid her head in her hands and blushed, and kept crying, saying over and over, "Oh, that was wicked! That was wicked! And now you won't love me anymore ... and now I'll be all alone ... "

I couldn't find a single tender word to console her. It seemed to me that I had lost my faculty of speech; it also seemed that everything had died in me, in that disillusioning act of love.

Chapter XXII

Écluses de Porte-Joie

Imagine a barren mountain peak, shaped in an amusingly long, thin cone. A few sickly trees cling to the summit, and their branches are adorned with pretty, decorative contorsions. Among these trees an old house sits crumbling, held up only by its vines of ivy. And all around it is the sky, the sky, a sky so immense it beggars the imagination. Well, now this comical peak, this house, this sky, it all belongs to me. I am, as of yesterday at eleven-thirty, the astonished and delighted proprietor. This is the great mystery unveiled!

This momentous event came off without too many snags. The dump had been up for sale for more than ten years. Nobody wanted it. I bought it for a crumb of bread, as that bleating Alfred de Musset put it. After dragging his heels a bit my father wound up giving me the funds required to accomplish this folly. Maybe he thought I was going to give up art for agriculture, and raise livestock on my mountainside. Anyway, I'm a landowner! And it seems hilarious to me. I don't think you'll recognize me. I'm convinced that I'm already getting a gut in honor of my new social standing, according to custom, and I've acquired that smugness so particular to "the man of property."

At the foot of the mountain are the locks of Porte-Joie that I told you about, and the admirable iron architecture of the dam that, from a distance, resembles immense nets stretched out in the sun atop the water. The population of Porte-Joie comprises an innkeeper, who's also a fisherman, his wife, and his domestic servant; a public engineer and his deputy; the weir-keeper, his wife, and his daughter; and an old retired captain. That's it! I guess there's also a fishing warden, who lurks around these parts all the time, and keeps an eye on the little salmon whose gestation the public engineer administrates in his hatcheries. But you couldn't really call this functionary part of the place. He lives on the other side of the river in a plank house, black with tar, with two poor sunflowers drooping in the front, beaten down by their environs. His real home, though, is the lounge at the inn, where, all day long, he absorbs the jugs of apple eau-de-vie that the innkeeper doles out generously, in the interest of spending the nights carting off fish without worrying about getting caught. Otherwise, the regulation of the game fish is admirable. It's forbidden to fish when there's anything to be caught; you're allowed to fish when there aren't any fish at all. At the moment, the shad are spawning. They go up the river in enormous shoals. Those fish have some strange customs. They'd rather die than return to the sea. And do they ever die! All you see on the river are the shining bellies of dead fish. It looks like a cascade of tiny icebergs. All right, so they forbid the river-dwellers and the fishermen to touch these fish. The administration, in their charity and fore-sight, allow only a small harvest once in a while, and it's to be given to the hospices hereabouts. Add to that the fact that when the livestock—cattle, calves or sheep—die, they too are sent to the same nursing homes, and you'll have an idea of the sort of diet—heavy as the feed that fat-tens the animals themselves—that they reserve for little old men, little old ladies, and pale convalescents.

Now, would you like to hear about of the morals and customs of my coinhabitants? They're very amusing.

The public engineer is sleeping with the innkeeper's wife; the innkeeper sleeps with the weir-keeper's wife; the weir-keeper is doing the innkeeper's servant; and the weir-keeper's daughter gets off with the public en-gineer's deputy. Everybody seems quite happy with it. There's just the old captain, who isn't sleeping with any-one. At least that's what they assume, and he concurs. The brave old soul replaces the joys of adultery and free love with an exclusive and violent passion for line fish-ing. He has, for this particular sport, devised a rational method, in the employment of which he never catches a fish. But he has faith in his doctrine, and the hope of future catches sustains him. He's a sort of apostle. And myself? I lord it over all the action from the heights of my peak.

My peak is an extraordinary one. There are spots where you can't see the earth, where you can see only the sky. I can imagine that I'm up in a balloon, in a per-petual climb toward the infinite. It's amazing. I've felt unheard-of sensations. Try to imagine it. All around me, the sky. No horizon, not a sound! Nothing but the silent march of the clouds. And suddenly, in this immeasurable void, in the silence of splendid eternities, the howl of a dog floats up from the invisible earth. First, the barking is faint, like a little cry; then, little by little, it intensifies till it sounds like a riot. And it goes on for entire days; and it goes on for whole nights. And it seems to me that it's the protest of man, the sound of mankind's revolt, taking arms against the sky; this crying dog, yes, it's the very voice of the earth. I don't know if you can understand what I'm trying to say . . . but the feeling, I assure you, is a bit terrifying.

Naturally, I haven't done any work. I'll have to get settled first, find a room for myself between these ruined walls—chase away the rats and the owls who, for centuries, have been leading their mysterious lives within them. All that will be promptly terminated. A bed, a table, two chairs, and my easels! And then, work! Work! I feel confident. It seems to me that I'm about to become a new man. Oh, to paint light, that light that comes from everywhere to bathe me! To paint the dramas of the light, the formidable life of the shadows! To seize and clasp that impalpable thing, to reach the unattainable! I'm full of enthusiasm; I feel new powers flowing through me . . . I want to kiss you, my dear boy, to tell you all that I hope for, to show you everything that's budding in my mind . . . you know that Turner painting? The one with, at the bottom of the canvas, there are floating shapes, russet and gold. You can't tell whether they're trees, scarves, faces, or clouds! . . . Then, at the top, there are deep whites, infinite, spiraling light. That's what I want to make, do you understand? Canvases with nothing on them! . . . Alright, but is that possible?

Yesterday, I spent the entire afternoon watching them unload a barge. It was a team of eight men. Ah! The bastards! How beautiful they were! The boat was filled with huge trees that they hefted as easily as I would pick up a pencil! The nobility of those torsos, the august splendor of those laboring muscles, and the rhythm of their hips, under their heavy loads, and the color of their velvet pants, cinched at the waist with a red belt! And from those blackened faces, hollowed by the fatigue of their overburdening work, came such innocent smiles! Yes, smiling like children, with muscles like Hercules! Ah, how they moved me! . . . That's beautiful too, you know . . . The power of these poor devils—I don't know quite what—it makes you tender, it almost makes you cry. How small everyone else seems next to these unlucky men! And right away they knew that I loved them. For me, they showed a thousand niceties, a thousand naïve gaieties, which charmed me.

In the evening, I paid for their drinks. We got a little ploughed together . . . it was delicious.

Why are you sad? Why despair so of your fate? One shouldn't be sad; you should always hope, because everything is beautiful, sacred goddamn son-of-a . . .

Many kisses.
Lucien.

Chapter XXIII

Lucien's letters went on like that, one overjoyed, the next broken-hearted. Each morning they brought me the echo of his soul. Through these letters I could follow, better perhaps than through our conversations of old, the progress of the blight that was invading him. That solitude, wherein he'd thought he could reclaim himself, in which he sought the calm required for mysterious creations, was to him dreadful and lethal instead. He lost himself in the desert of that silence, even more so than in the Parisian racket that he'd fled; his soul wasn't strong enough to carry the weight of that huge and heavy sky, where no paths were traced. And already, dismal signs announced the madness that would later drown the ardent and incomplete intelligence of my friend.

There on my table, I have those letters, which I can't re-read without tears, or without a terrible tremor shaking me from my head to my feet. They seem to have been written by a condemned man. From the first line to the last, they express the most awful torment at the hand of Art that a man can suffer on this earth. I've spent much time reflecting on these things, and I can't stop myself from thinking that this suffering was just and deserved. It isn't good for a man to distance himself too far from life, because life will have its revenge.

"Fancy this," he wrote. "This morning I made an important discovery. While I was putting on my pants, I realized that the back side of the fabric was far more attractive than the front. It's that way with everything— not just in the material realm, in fact, but above all in the moral realm! Think deeply on this fact. You can't hope to know truth and beauty but through the back side of things. And the back side of life is death. I want to die, and finally know the truth and beauty of life!"

And the next day, he wrote to me again:

"Without a doubt, I have been wrong. I've often had the arrogance to believe that I was, or that I could become, an artist. I was insane. I'm nothing, nothing but a useless sower of dead seeds. Nothing grows—nothing will ever grow—from the seeds that I am weary and disgusted to have thrown into the wind, like the sad and sterile Onan. These seeds of art and life—one could say that the touch of my hand is enough to rot them in the bud! Oh! This feeling of powerlessness, the accursed power of death! It pursues me even into my sleep! Every night I have this strange and agonizing nightmare: I'm a gardener, and I'm planting lilies. As I bear it closer to the earth, the lily bulb, powerful and beautiful like a phallus, wilts in my hand; its scales peel away, rotten and sticky, and when I try at last to push it into the soil, the bulb has disappeared. All my dreams bear the same stamp of abortion, rot, and death! I wake up panting, my body bathed in sweat, and I leave my bed to escape that awful sleep, that atrocious dream, where my own disintegration comes out in force!

But if I'm not an artist, then what am I? And what should I do? In truth, I don't know. I'm no good for any job; nature has cursed me. Could I push a harrow, carry heavy loads? My back is too weak. Could I teach men, preaching beauty? But men don't understand anything. They're too old. Teach children? Talk to little ones, whose heads haven't been hardened by experience, whose minds haven't yet been calcified by education? Alas, when I find myself before a child, I don't know what to say! I think children have things sussed better than I, they're wise to everything. Often, a very old, poor man comes by here begging—very old and poor, practically blind, and he's led by his granddaughter, who's mute. And the gaze of this mute girl is infinitely frightening! It looks like her eyes have seen all, known all. They're vast like a sky and deep as an abyss, from the thickest shadows to the most resplendent light. Before this gaze, which has never registered anything men say—before that closed mouth, that virginal flower of a mouth, that not one human word has soiled—I feel most small, most humble, utterly stupid, trembling like a dog before its master!

I kept them here for a few days, the old blind man and the little mute ... In that time I soiled more than ten canvases. I wanted to express, do you understand, to render, through a combination of lines and forms, everything a blind man can see, and everything a mute girl can say. And nothing! Nothing came of it! My hand refused to paint what I felt, what I understood so well from the inside, all the emotion that filled my soul before that firmamental gaze, before that astral mouth . . . do you understand? Ah, if I'd had a cleaver, I swear to you that I'd have cut off my hand, and I would've taken a diabolical joy in nailing that imbecilic hand to my work-shop door as an object of derision!"

And here is the final letter that I received from Lucien:

"I'm letting you know, dear boy, that three days from now I'll be returning to Paris. I need to go back there to look for some furnishings that I need. But more than that, I need to talk to you, with some others, with everyone. Here, by myself, I'm suffocating. It's too beautiful for me, too big . . . I lose myself in the sky as though it were a virgin forest. Too many things go on in the air that we don't understand . . . there are too many flowers, too many plains, too many forests, too many terrible seas . . . everything becomes indistinguishable. The forests float like oceans, the seas dishevel like forests, and the flowers put me to sleep with their poisons. And they unleash a great madness, and a great terror. I would need someone else near me, to understand this formidable beauty with me, to rejoice in it together. And I have no one to take up the overflow of what's boiling over within me. We can come back together to my peak, if you'd like, if there's nothing new that ties you to Paris, as must be the case, I believe. You must be lonely too."

And sure enough, three days after that letter, Lucien returned to Paris. He embraced me exuberantly.

"Oh! Sweet little one!" he kept saying, "How good it feels to see you again . . . "

He was altered, paler, thinner. His long hair and wild beard gave his face an even more ruined look. His eyes burned with a feverish luster.

"Are you ill?" I asked uneasily.

"Ill? And why? No, I'm not sick, I'm tired. Out there, I wasn't sleeping anymore. But here, I'm going to sleep really well."

He went by to inspect his workshop and looked at a few of his old studies, not without pleasure.

"Say! Well, that one isn't too bad, there!"

And abruptly:

"You know . . . one never knows what can happen . . . I've made out my will; I'm giving you my mountain. Let's go have dinner . . . and then, by god! Afterward we should go out and get ourselves some women . . . let's go! Come on! We must have a few kicks tonight!"

Chapter XXIV

As we left the bordello where we'd gone to get our kicks, Lucien, filled with shame, said to me:

"God, are we ever stupid! And what the hell were we doing there, I ask you?! I was cheerful earlier, happy to be back, to see you again . . . I don't know, happy for the change of place . . . and now look at me, sadder than the dead! Not to mention that tomorrow I won't be able to work—my mind will still be incapacitated by this filth! So is that what pleasure is?!"

He spat on the ground and went on:

"To think that there are people who think only of that, who do only that! People for whom all of life boils down to that instant of deceptive and ridiculous bliss! There are poets who take such fetid buttocks for a wishing star! To think that people work, steal, kill, only for that! Do you know why I've never had any friends, not one except you? It's because all the young men I might have possibly liked had to stuff their tales of erotic prowess down my throat! But, damn it! There's more to life than sloshing your flesh over the flesh of some soiled, swooning female!"

And he seemed to take the night for a witness, the

sparkling sky, the mystery of the shadows between the shimmering lights that flickered and flapped over the buildings like thin scarves lifted by a light breeze.

"Because, in the end, did you enjoy yourself?! Let's see! Did you feel in your loins the marvelous tremor that opens the doors of paradise? What a joke! What a dirty joke! . . . But, on the other hand, those cathouses are quite amusing . . . one should go there strictly as a painter though, not for idiot pleasure! What ruins the powerful strangeness, the macabre splendor of such a spectacle, is the mindless act to which you feel duty-bound to sacrifice yourself! That riot of colors, the midden of raw poverty, those shreds of flesh and transparent cloth that multiply in the mirrors! And what one glimpses through the open doors, in the somber red stairways—a nude torso passing by, a pasty thigh caught in flight, cut by the line of a door curtain; tangled masses of red locks, and the apparition of those plaster-white faces, made up like the Egyptian dead . . . Ah, to capture the sadness, the shocking and scarlet sadness of such a public auction! The anguish that takes you at the sight of all that meat, dressed, washed, and decorated with fake flowers like a display on a butcher's table! It's beautiful, oh yes, it's beautiful! But all the same, I prefer real flowers, the fog on the hills—all those dreams of purity, of a colorful, limpid atmosphere, whose marvelous fairy tricks veil the bitter reality of life . . . Look, how about you, do women amuse you? Are you going to go off like the others and drown yourself in the white flowers of love? Why aren't you saying anything?"

He was shaking me roughly by the shoulders.

I responded with an evasive laugh, and Lucien didn't push any further. His thoughts were already wandering elsewhere.

"You'll see my mountain," he said suddenly, with no transition. "Because I think you're going to come with me. And because I'm giving it to you in my will, of course you'll have to see it. We'll both be really happy, that's one thing for sure. What disoriented me a bit was being alone, never being able to talk to anybody. I need to cry out with my ideas; without that, my work is intolerable suffering. I have to empty myself of everything that oppresses me. If I don't—it's curious—my hand trembles, I can't even hold a damn paintbrush. And you'll really love my mountaintop; it's covered with admirable flowers, willowherb with their flexible bells, doronica and inulae—and on the walls, those crumbling old walls, there are falls, cascades, cataracts of succulents! We can bring along sunflower seeds, and sow them all along the fields . . . can't you just see it now, those great, wild flowers, full-blown in the sky! And then maybe you'll give me some advice on my painting! Do you remember, I told you about that dog who bays endlessly, a dog you can't see, and whose voice rises toward the sky, like the very voice of the earth? That's what I want to do! A vast sky . . . and the cry of that dog!"

I was a bit taken aback. "But you're insane, Lucien! You want to paint the bark of a dog?"

"Yes! Yes! It's possible! Anything is! . . . you have to find it, that's all! Like this, see, for example, a rising spiral...ah, I don't know...or a cloud that would be lower than the others, shaped like a dog, like a dog's mouth! Understand me...what I want would be to show, with nothing but light, with nothing but aerial, floating forms, that would make you feel infinity, space without limit, the celestial abyss; it would be to paint everything that groans, everything that cries, all that suffers on the earth...the invisible inside the untouchable..."

"Lucien! Lucien! I beg you, don't talk like that, it scares me..."

I was appalled. In the half-light where we walked, I thought I saw strange, unbearable lights leering in Lucien's eyes and on his lips, and he said in a flat voice:

"Dear boy, when you've seen what happens in that sky, well! You'll tell me a thing or two...you haven't seen anything yet...you haven't understood a thing..."

We returned home. I didn't feel like sleeping, and after rummaging awhile in his boxes, Lucien asked me, "Did you do any work, at least? Read me something."

He wouldn't leave me alone till I read him a few pages of a new work I'd started a hundred times and abandoned just as often.

Then he himself interrupted my reading: "That's enough! That's enough!" he said. "I don't know anything about literature...but I've got my ideas about it, like anyone...would you like to hear what I think? It's worthless. It's too straightforward...you're for the School of Two Plus Two Makes Four!"

Although in my own opinion these lines, written

with such difficulty, were meritless indeed, I felt hurt at having it put to me so brutally.

"Ah, so what have we here?" said Lucien. "A bit of pride! That's the living end! Ah! My poor little imbecile! But get this into your head: Art isn't there to establish that two and two make four. Art is made only to ferret out the beauty hidden beneath things. What good is it to write what everybody knows? Any vaudevillian and his carny barker are going to beat you at that game. Be obscure, for Christ's sake! Obscurity is art's finest attire ... and its dignity as well! Only boors and professors write clearly. That's because they've never realized that everything is a mystery, that the mysterious can't be expressed like a pun or a marriage contract. Is nature clear? It's about time you came up to my peak and investigated the sky! There's where you'll find truth and beauty ... "

He stood up and added: "I've had enough of Paris ... we're leaving tomorrow."

Chapter XXV

Lucien didn't leave the next day, as we'd agreed. He dawdled at pointless errands, went to revisit friends, to see the quays that had inspired him; he found a thousand pretexts to put off the moment of his departure—of our departure, rather, as he'd decided that I would go with him to spend a few days on his peak ... and curiosity did compel me toward this new suffering-ground of his. Anyway, Lucien was in such a state of unhealthy excitement that I was afraid all kinds of things might happen to him if he were left alone, to live constantly withdrawn into himself, with only the madness inhabiting his soul for company. I would have felt too guilty to leave him to his vertigo; I wanted to watch over him, like you watch someone who's ill. While I was waiting, I followed everywhere he went; I was like his shadow, like the shadow of his shadow. Meanwhile he exhausted himself with talk, theories, and wild gestures. It was a rumbling flux of memories and plans, mixed with tales of strange sensations, sketches of landscapes, schemes for social reform, scraps of nature, humanity, and dreams—vague, breathless, agitated things, unrelated to each other, like things glimpsed at night through the side door of a wagon tied to a locomotive that's taking it who knows where, at full steam ahead.

We spent an entire day at the Louvre, and I'll never forget how Lucien fell apart when the museum closed and we went out toward the Tuileries. The end of that day was radiant. The falling sun made the stands of trees look weightless, cloudy, and the rectangle of the Arc de Triomphe rose up, washed in blue by the light of the western sky, blue outlined with a ray of orange light. The streets were a backdrop to a thousand things that glowed and shimmered; coaches like jewels, dresses like flowers . . . we fell onto a bench. I was edgy with fatigue, my head empty and my eyes burning; he was stark and silent and reminded me of some poor devil who'd been overcome by hunger and a road that was too long. He leaned his head on his hands and blew twisted streams of saliva at the ground. I'd never seen him so thin, so fleshless. His protruding shoulder blades seemed to tear the rumpled cloth of his jacket like nails. In his lumpy black hat, with his overgrown beard and hair, he looked like a beggar, or like one of those sad bohemians whom he'd once taken such pleasure in mocking—he had always been so sharp, in his bourgeois and almost elegant dress.

Suddenly, he said:

"Do you see, dear boy, in art, there's only one thing that's great and beautiful: Health! As for me, I'm sick, and my illness is terrible; and now I'm too old to cure myself . . . It's ignorance. Yes, I don't know the first thing about my art, and I never will know a thing! I'm not insane, as you might suppose—I'm a weakling, which is quite different. Or, if you prefer, a failure … Do you know why I drive myself to find out all these complicated things, what others call "rarefied sensations," and which aren't anything but children's games, and lies … Do you know why? It's because I'm incapable of painting what's simple! Because I don't know how to draw, and I don't know how to render the shadows and the light! So I replace them with arabesques, and embellishments, by a mess of perversions of forms that only fool imbeciles! And, since I can't paint a fellow standing on his legs, I put him in standing on his head. They say, "Oh, that's amazing!" But no, I'm a pig, plain and simple! Go look at painters like your Terburghs, your Metsus, Rembrandt—did they try to paint the bark of a dog? They simply painted men and women. And they were right! … And how about Père Corot? Did he try to paint trees with their roots in the air? And whirling stars that look shit-faced drunk? No! And he was right! Ah, they've done me wrong, those aesthetes of misery, with their flowery voices, preaching hatred for nature, love of grotesque coloring, telling us we don't need to know how to draw, rolling art backward to embryonic forms, to the existence of a larva! Because isn't that exactly the ideal with which they've poisoned an entire generation? Ah! Their princesses, with beanpole bodies and faces that look like poisonous flowers, descending staircases made of clouds, strolling the terraces of sickly moons, with dresses like a peacock's tail. Or a feather duster! Their saints, emaciated and elongated like a fishing pole—their courtesans walking along with no legs, staring without eyes, talking without a mouth, loving with no sex organ, and who, under greenery that looks like it's been stamped out by a machine, caress hands that are as flat as palm branches and always in the same cliched pose, like their wrists are broken! And their heros, who stink of pederasty... necrosis... syphilis! Their greenish flesh; the stench of those flowers that look like they've been dunked in bloody bidet water! Bah! I never believed in that impoverished art, in that low mysticism, and yet, little by little, without knowing it, I let myself be taken in, be invaded, by all these false theories that corrode the air we breathe, we young men, who long for novelty and are easily made to believe that the bizarre is the beautiful! Instead of working methodically, learning to draw a beautiful movement from nature, a pretty living form, looking for what's simple and great, I wound up thinking that irritation and deformity was art! And look where I am now! I'm screwed! I have a profession, but I don't know how to do it. So now what? ... "

He straightened up a bit on the bench, and with a feverish trembling hand he drew straight lines and squares in the sand.

"Look! Do you know why these days they make furniture that's so prodigiously ugly, loaded down with hideous sculptures and ornmaments that make a man of taste ill? Ah, my god, it's only because the carpenters no longer know their trade. They can no longer plane a pretty line, nor establish a beautiful harmony of proportions . . . so they smother you with decorations! And yet a table with no molding, nothing but the plain line, is quite pretty, wouldn't you say? Oh, but that's too hard! I'm like the carpenters! It's only to hide my impotence that I go chasing after the crazy things that I'm dying of! . . . Because you know, my dear boy, I'm dying of them! Or, rather, I'm croaking like an animal. Oh! To make beautiful healthy art, like Père Corot . . . or even like Claude Monet, like Camille Pissarro! Isn't their painting wonderful as well? In the admirable equilibrium of their minds, don't you feel the enthusiasm, the eternal youth of poetry, the ardor of the creative imagination? And they know! They're great workmen. Ah, to know!"

"Well, so couldn't you restrict yourself to working methodically?" I said to Lucien. "If you think you don't know enough, couldn't you learn? . . . I think you could do it . . . You can keep your imagination, your passions . . . because those things are what make you . . . But if you force yourself to do simple work, as you're copying the forms of nature, you'll develop the technique that you're missing . . . And then later you can realize all the things you dream . . . "

"No! It's too late . . . The poison is in my blood, in my muscles. It's paralyzed my hand . . . I can't do it anymore! I can't do anything! I'm ruined!"

And after a moment of silence:

"Go back there? I'm going to go crazier than ever in the enormity of my sky! Oh, yes, I'm terrified of that sky! . . . But stay here? But all day long, I'll hear those accursed voices honking in my ears: 'Lilies! Lilies! Lilies!'"[1]

Lucien stood up and beat at the air with his cane, and to the great estonishment of a gentleman who was passing by, he thundered:

"Lilies! Lilies! What shit!"

---

1   Lilies were a favorite subject of the Pre-Raphaelite painters; a typical treatment appears in Dante Gabriel Rossetti's *Ecce Ancilla Domini* ("Here comes God's personal assistant!" or *The Annunciation*) (1850). As evidenced by this and other passages—such as in the very similar short story "DES LYS! DES LYS!," published in *Le Journal* during the month of April 1895, almost exactly two years after this and the surrounding chapters appeared in *L'Écho de Paris*—Mirbeau was not overwhelmingly fond of this school of painting.

Chapter XXVI

All these little incidents that conspired to turn my life upside down were pushing me away from Julia. I almost never saw her anymore; I only got glimpses through the curtains of her lodge, where her sad face would appear to me, like a little plant yellowing in the shade. She wilted more and more; her hair took on the somber hue of a sick animal's fur, and her red-rimmed eyes blinked like an anaemic chicken's. She really did touch my heart, but that emotion couldn't overcome the disgust, the pitiful and painful disgust for her, that I suffered after the physical act that drowned my love, and all the poetry of my love. The pot of cineraria had been succeeded by a pot of gillyflowers. That was the one event that had slightly altered the monotony of that melancholy hovel. The woman and the flower were both so faded, their fates were so similar, that I came to confuse them in the same vegetative poverty; and when I passed by the lodge and saw the two pale drooping shapes, I really could no longer say which was the flower and which the woman.

Once I had an errand in the lodge that I couldn't avoid, and I found Julia there alone. She gave me a look so imploring, so depressingly imploring, that it stabbed at the bottom of my soul. And I damned myself for the cruelty of my conduct toward this poor girl, whom I'd seduced and then abandoned out of cowardice. But I believe that into that surge of pity there stole a feeling of pride, and—bastard that I am—I compared myself to some terrible Don Juan.

"Are you really leaving?" Julia asked, humble and afraid.

As I hesitated shamefully to respond, she added, with more spirit: "It's Monsieur Lucien who told me that!"

I was terrified that she had told Lucien our little tale, which I wanted hidden at all costs. I think I would have died of shame if Lucien knew. All my pity evaporated and I replied coldly: "Oh! So Lucien told you! I'll bet you went and told him a pack of lies!"

"Lies?!" she cried. "Oh, you're so rotten! Why are you so cruel to me? I didn't tell Monsieur Lucien anything. He just came and told me. He told me he was leaving again, and that he was bringing you with him! Is it true?"

She was sincere. Her anxious regard brought the pity back again:

"Yes, Julia, it's true . . . "

"Oh! My God! What about me? What will I be without you?"

She couldn't hold back the tears brimming in her swollen eyes.

"Oh! My God! Oh, my God!" she sobbed. "I had nothing left but you! And you're going away! And I'll be all alone . . . and I'm going to die all alone! I could tell you didn't love me anymore . . . "

I tried to console her; I took her poor thin hands, their veins knotted like little blue strings.

"Look, Julia. It's true, I'm going to leave ... but it's only for a few days. Lucien is depressed and ill. I have to go with him ... but I'll be back soon."

"Easy to say! Easy to say!"

"I promise you ... Oh, come on, don't cry. I swear it to you. Come on, I swear it!"

But she sighed and shook her head, and squeezed my hand in a damp grip that I could barely stand.

"Easy to say! It's just so many words!"

"I assure you, I won't be there long! We'll come back really soon."

"No! No! You won't come back at all! Because Monsieur Lucien is crazy! He's insane! Everyone knows he's insane ... and he'll make you crazy too! And you won't come back ... "

I didn't know what more to say.

"I'll leave you some books, Julia, some beautiful books. And then I'll write you some letters, beautiful letters, and then you'll write back beautiful letters too! And then we'll see each other soon ... "

She clung closer; her clawlike hand clamped around my arm, went up my shoulder, wrapped itself around my throat; her pale mouth, uncovering its tartar-caked teeth, opened as if to kiss me; and her eyes watched mine darting about the little room where, on the fire, that eternal broth simmered. I was looking for an escape; I turned my head to avoid the warm, stale breath, the sick-smelling breath that came at me from her mouth.

"Don't leave," she groveled. "Please, please, don't leave yet . . . be nice, my sweet, my big strong darling . . . don't leave me alone anymore . . . don't believe whatever Monsieur Lucien told you . . . please . . . "

The broth bubbled; above the earthen pot rose tiny spirals of vapor. And I was terrified by those two rancid odours—that gross soup, and that female.

Suddenly Julia let out a little cry, and let fall the arms she had twined around me.

"Ah! What a nuisance!" she said. At that moment, a step had sounded in the vestibule. And the postman appeared. I took advantage of that liberating respite and took off. It was time.

That same day Lucien, very chipper, came back to the workshop around noon. Under his arm he had a long basket covered with a grey cloth.

"Guess what's in there," he said, placing the basket on the ground. "Look . . . it's moving . . . it's alive! So c'mon, guess!" He gave a hearty laugh, charming and artless, like in the old days. A childish, happy look played on his tormented face like the light of dawn. "You're not guessing, little imbecile!"

Without waiting for my reply, he cut the strings that tied the cloth to the basket; the cloth flew up and in a great rush of wings a peacock appeared.

"Oh, the bastard, how beautiful he is!" Lucien cheered.

The peacock stretched, fluffed its feathers, shook out its wings, with their fine embroidery of scales. It swept the floor with its long tail, like a woman swirling the train of her dress; then, with its neck proudly erect, its crest thrown back and trembling, it paraded around the chamber with the majesty of a Hindu divinity. And then suddenly it jumped up on the fireplace, where it sat down, letting its tail fall with a rustle of gold and strange jewels that filled the room. From above its blue ruff, whose swirling iridescence danced in a ray of sun, it stared at us with its black pearl of an eye, a pearl mounted in a double ring of white and black velour.

"So?' said Lucien, "What do you think of him? Do you think he's decorative enough?"

"What are you doing with a peacock?" I said.

'What am I doing with him? What, I didn't tell you? Hm, I've been dreaming of it for a long time . . . well then, here you are! I thought of a great motif: A group of peacocks . . . on a field of pansies. No, but, well, do you get the idea!? The peacocks lying in the pansies, walking in pansies . . . and perhaps, bordering the field of pansies, near the top of the canvas, some poppies . . . no, wait, no poppies! That I'll save for another piece . . . some peacocks gliding through poppies!"

And his gestures, drawing long tails of the peacocks and the stems of plants in the air, orchestrated his words; his whole face lit up with joy.

"I believe," he said, "that I finally have hold of something astounding! And you know . . . there's no pastiche in it . . . no atmosphere . . . not any more! Just peacocks drawn feather by feather, and exaggerated . . . exaggerated! Look!"

He traced great lines with his finger.

"Let's go! No more joking! No more stupidity! This, I

feel! This is mine! And tomorrow, to work! Aw, but look at that peacock—is this animal posing for me?"

"So, we're not leaving?" I asked Lucien.

My friend looked at me vaguely.

"Leaving? And why would we be going? And where?"

"But—to our mountain peak! Out there . . ."

Lucien reflected for a second.

"Our mountain! Oh! yes . . . But you're crazy, I think."

And from his pocket he pulled a packet of kernels of corn, which he threw one by one to the peacock on the hearth.

"Eat, my little fellow, eat, my coco! Little one! Little one!"

Chapter XXVII

Lucien attacked his work with gusto. By the next morning already, when I entered the workshop, I saw that malignant wrinkle on his forehead, the crease that would appear when he was incubating an idea, harbinger of the storms to come. And I couldn't help but be afraid. In his renewed confidence, in the hot peals of his laughter, there was a discordant note that made me uneasy. Nor did I like that to see him jumping around so abruptly that he made enough wind to blow his hair back; it made his face look crazier.

"Don't get so feverish about the work," I told him. "You've got time, calm down."

"Jesus Christ! How can you be calm when you're working!? That's fine for you! You can afford booze! But can you tell a fire not to burn? Do you say to the wind, 'Don't blow?' It's fire and wind that I have in my head— it burns and it roars!"

In the mornings, Lucien starting going to a horticulturer's place in Montrouge to make studies of pansies, of fields of pansies. When he came back, he recounted his impressions with bizarre metaphors.

"There was one, imagine it, that looked like a tiger . . . another—oh, that one! No, it's too awful . . . imagine the head of a corpse growing out of the earth on a slender stalk . . . I looked at it . . . the base was dead, it hadn't put out a leaf . . . nothing but that terrifying flower! Do you understand that? The gardener I showed it to just shrugged his shoulders . . . what a brute! These people, they don't see anything!"

In the afternoons, straight through till evening, he drew his peacock. He made sad peacocks, drunken peacocks, crazy ones, dead ones; he made them in all possible shapes, all colors, every pose. The live peacock quickly made himself at home. He no longer lurked along the wall swinging his head back and forth, looking for a way to escape; he quit throwing himself against the window panes that let him see, over the forest, the chimneys and the stove-pipes, liberty in a corner of the sky . . . He accepted with good grace the narrowness of the room and the perch we'd improvised for him from an old easel; he was content with the sad greenery, the bunches of weeds and dandelions, that Lucien made sure to strew the parquet with every night to give the bird the illusion of a garden. The peacock even began to strike poses and make gestures that animals ordinarily refuse to display when they can feel humans watching them. Most of all, when he was cleaning himself, he had a resplendent manner of lifting and spreading his magical tail that sent Lucien into transports of delirious joy.

It took more than two weeks of studies and sketches to prepare for Lucien's great work of dreams, and he was happy the whole time. His enthusiasm, buoyed by hope, didn't flag for a minute. Though the furrow in his forehead got deeper all the time, hollowing out like a wound, presaging terrible storms, those cyclones of rage that I, alas, knew all too well, he radiated confidence.

"Rest a little," I advised him. "You can't keep working so furiously for long . . . and everything's going to start all over like it did before, you know that. Don't exhaust yourself— please!"

But he didn't listen to me.

"I'm perfectly calm, as you can well see," he said. "I'm strong . . . I've never felt so supple before . . . and yet I've improved . . . "

What astonished me most was that he tolerated having me near him while he worked. Before, he would show me the door, saying gaily:

"I'm like an elephant! I'm a prude . . . I don't like anybody watching me fornicate with art!"

Now he not only tolerated me, he seemed reassured by my presence, and he often asked my opinion about his studies, trying to probe my true thoughts, like a doctor examining a patient, looking deep into my eyes.

"Not there yet, eh? No, not yet! Tell me frankly . . . say what you think . . . but I think that it has to, all the same—oh yes! It's in there!"

He pointed at his forehead; then, playing with the sinews of his fingers as though to relax them he added, with a hiss in his voice that made me shiver:

"It's just this damned hand that still won't obey! This damned hand, always rebelling against what I feel, against what I want . . . "

And he'd go on swearing at it.

"I have to break you, you whore! You have to work like the rest of me, you pig, you pig, you fucking pig!"

Finally, one morning he began to wrestle his design onto the big canvas.

It was a very long canvas, not very tall. The peacocks went the entire length of the fabric, moving strangely and superbly; and not one of them, despite the apparent symmetry of the composition, looked like another. Before and behind the peacocks there stretched a marvelous tapestry, a field of pansies that the frame cut off at every side. The effect was arresting . . . it was a powerful, beautiful work of the imagination, a unison of linear harmony and ornamentation that I admired without restraint.

"My god, that's beautiful, Lucien!"

But already Lucien was shaking his head . . . and his eye, boring into the canvas, grew more disturbed.

"Why do you tell me it's beautiful? Do you know if it is? Do you know something I don't? Well, I think it's not right! I'll never be able to find the right harmony between these peacocks, these birds who are like flowers, and the flowers that are so much like the birds . . . it's lacking an element, maybe . . . oh, yes, it's missing something . . . a nude figure, a woman . . . right there. Yes! A figure styled just like the decor, with red tresses . . . with hair of gold that would flow over the canvas like another peacock's tail."

"Leave your idea as you first dreamed it, Lucien—I'm telling you, it's beautiful! The beauty is palpable ... you'd ruin everything with all that hair."

As the canvas edged toward completion, as Lucien filled in each bird in studied detail against the softer background, his mad doubts returned, stronger than ever. One day, brusquely, he turned on me and cried:

"Most of all, it's you that bothers me! I feel you, always there, behind me ... you ruin my thoughts ... get out of here, you weigh on my shoulders! Leave me alone ... "

I withdrew without arguing, and my heart was heavy. I knew that at such moments it was worse than useless to try to calm my friend with words. But I didn't want to leave him; I felt God knew what misery drawing near. I stayed on the landing of the stairs. I spent my days on that landing, waiting at that somber door, beyond which poor Lucien lived in battle with the demon of art. And with my ear tuned to the smallest sound, I heard his brush tapping on the canvas; I heard the hoarse curses, which the peacock, from time to time, would answer with a scream.

Chapter XXVIII

I lived among the shadows of that landing for days, cruel, painful days that seemed long, so long they seemed to never end. My ear was glued to the door, and I listened to every sound with horrible anguish, and my heart would convulse at the slightest creak of the floor. The staircase ended at this ultimate landing, and the landing formed a black recess from which extended a sordid corridor that was lit by a small skylight, and at the end of the corridor was my room. On a wooden board, in a corner between two doors, stood a kerosene lamp that was never lit, and intolerable odors circulated, rancid, poisonous smells that drifted down from the ceiling, rose up the stairs, and oozed from the walls, which were crawling with black insects that swarmed strangely. I didn't dare move or walk in the corridor, afraid that Lucien would hear me. He wouldn't have tolerated me hovering there like a watchdog. And he would have been really angry at me for spying on him like that, because he wouldn't have understood the sentiment that moved me to it—a feeling of tenderness multiplied tenfold by fear. But a secret instinct warned me that I should watch over him despite himself, despite anything. I felt something weighing on the air around my friend, something tragic, something that was prowling, fierce and terrible; perhaps it was death. And I told myself I could protect him, that as long as I was there I could chase away the pain and danger.

Often, Julia would escape the lodge for a few minutes to run up and see me. She got there out of breath, panting, paler than ever from her hasty efforts, her dull blond locks pasted to her forehead with sweat. Nothing annoyed me like these repeated visits, her obsessed eyes, where I read of a haunting love that was becoming burdensome and odious to me. She loved the darkness that was conducive to her desires; she sought out the shadows; she wanted to drag me into the darkness with her every time. When I heard her coming, when I heard her old shoes slipping and clopping up the stairs, rising up toward me, I would go over to the stairwell where we would both resign ourselves to having a bizarre debate.

"No, Julia," I would tell her firmly. "You have to go back downstairs. It's not a good idea to leave your apartment like that . . . what if your mother came back? What kind of situation would that put me in?"

"Give me just a minute with you . . . "

"No! Get out of here."

"Why don't you go into Monsieur Lucien's room? Are you angry with him?"

"No, I'm not angry with Lucien . . . Lucien is sick."

And then we'd hear him swearing through the door, a curse that he stifled as though it were a sob.

"Why is he swearing?" asked Julia.

"Because he's suffering!"

"Oh, that tells me a lot. And why does he suffer?"

"Because he's working."

"He's working! Great, that explains it."

"Let it go, Julia. Let me be."

But she wouldn't go away.

"Ah! how can you sit there all day, waiting at the door of a madman? . . . I would die of fright!"

"I will not let you call Lucien crazy."

"Right, so he's not crazy?"

"You're the one who's an idiot! . . . . Go away."

"Well! I'm telling you he is crazy! Yesterday, Mother was cleaning his studio and she saw that big painting he's making! Well! Mother said that Monsieur Lucien was crazy. He doesn't even know what he's painting anymore. Mother also said we need to get rid of the peacock, because it bothers the tenants, screaming all the time, the dirty beast . . . So, what, you don't think a man who has a peacock in his room is crazy?"

"Be quiet!"

"You know what else is true . . . "

She just kept going.

"You know what else is true? When Lucien wasn't here, you were nice to me. Since he came back, you won't even look at me anymore. First off, that guy, you know everyone knows he doesn't like girls . . . "

It took all the trouble in the world for me to get rid of Julia and her chatter. And when she left, I resumed my motionless watch . . . And as I sat in the dark without moving, barely even breathing, it seemed I was guarding a dead man.

One day, looking crazed and afraid, palette in hand, with paint smeared all over him, Lucien lurched out of his room and started rummaging around in the darkness:

"Damn it! When are they going to leave me in peace?"

I didn't have time to flee toward the corridor, so Lucien saw me standing there against the wall . . .

"Oh, it is you, you silly animal? And what are you doing here? Why are you here?"

"I was going home, Lucien . . . "

"I forbid you to spy on me. Do you hear? All day long, I've been bothered by the rats that were gnawing away behind my door . . . So, it was you!"

"Lucien! Lucien!"

"Leave me alone!"

"Lucien, I beg of you . . . Don't work so hard? It's making you sick . . . "

He slammed the door brusquely in my face. And I heard him pacing around his studio for a long time afterward, hissing . . .

The next day, I arrived at my post later than usual; I hadn't been able to sleep during the night, but when morning came an invincible sleep had kept me in bed as if I'd been tied down with ropes of lead. Behind the door, there was no sound: neither the brush tapping on the canvas, nor the creaking of the easel. I put my ear against the lock. Usually I could even hear Lucien breathing; barely a second went by when I didn't hear his feet pacing on the parquet, or an oath coming from his mouth, or at least the peacock walking and shaking its feathers. But now a deathly silence reigned behind the door. At first I assumed that Lucien was tired and had not yet risen. But the silence grew more and more disturbing till it finally made me panic. Suddenly, without thinking about the consequences of such audacity, I pushed against the door and yelled:

"Lucien! Lucien!"

No voice responded to my cry, and the door wouldn't budge.

I cried again:

"Lucien! . . . Lucien!"

And, kicking and punching, I tried to break down the door, that terrible door, the door behind which the silence grew more terrifying and sinister every second.

The neighbors began to appear in the hall, frightened by my howling.

"Lucien is dead! Lucien is dead!" I cried. "Oh, please, help me break down this door . . . "

In a minute, the door yielded to our efforts. In the middle of the workshop lay the great canvas, overturned and bashed in; nearby was the peacock, with its neck broken, dead; and by the peacock lay Lucien, in a sea of blood, his beard matted with red clots, his eyes open mad and wide, his mouth open in a horrible grin . . .

"Lucien! Lucien!" I cried.

I threw myself on his cold cadaver; I tried to hold him, make him sit up, rewarm him . . . and then I saw his hand . . . his right hand was detached at the wrist, sawed off, bloodless, with a ruined, twisted little hacksaw still stuck in it.

"Ah, so that's what I was hearing all night!" said one neighbor. "There was an incredible racket upstairs from me."

"Oh yeah . . . I remember now. Somebody was singing all night," said another.

And a third added:

"Yes, I heard someone sawing at something for hours!"

And I fainted.

Translator's Note

Learn French if you really want to read Mirbeau. Learn Russian if you feel that strongly about *The Idiot*. Translation is a miserable thing.

Then again, this injunction ignores the main problem with a translation from the nineteenth century: *time.* The past is an unyieldingly exclusive set of countries that we can never even visit, much less become fluent in the local parlance. My dear modern Anglophone, can you even read Shakespeare and really get the shade of every word?

Ftt, I can't. It's hard enough for two sisters to tell each other how they feel in the secret language they've known from the common den. How is a modern person going to tell another modern person what a prodigy manipulating words a hundred and fifteen years ago was trying to say? —And without sounding like a crazy old foreigner?

The first problem is to not make the translation sound like a sexually frustrated Martian trying to speak Earth languages. In other words you can't translate things too literally; I'm trying to show you how good

Mirbeau was, ideally, not how well I know nineteenth century French. (Good thing, since that body of knowledge would fail to impress a speech-impeded hamster.)

Then again, wading too deep into the waters that make the translation flow can easily fall into rewriting, and writing over the author.

There are some things you can say in perfectly natural French that you can barely approximate using even the most contorted English; that's the nature of the beast. All languages are incomplete—otherwise painters, like the antihero Lucien of the story you've just read, would have no reason to put brush to canvas (or whatever it is that visual artists do now). And so the translation monkey must, once in a while, just let the translation sound . . . weird.

But to call this a "language barrier" only marks the gap between two contemporaries. What would you call the other gap I'm translating here? The time cliff is by far the largest obstacle to "good" (insofar as it can be) translation. It's one thing to turn modern French into modern English; they're both stuffed with slang and obscenity, so one *fuck* in the hand is worth three *merdes* in the bush; screw it.

It's another to translate any previous era to the mass assumptions that our global interhorde makes about narrative and dialogue. What do I do about the fact that Mirbeau's characters keep on saying "oh!" where we would *merdefuck*—or, worse, the fact that he writes paragraphs that are longer than our attention span for the entire day?

Well, fuck it.

I let Mirbeau have his lack of unchained obscenity, except where it seemed his relatively genteel nineteenth century characters were so broken down they lapsed into ancestral coarseness; once upon a time, if only for a time, people could accept expression of deep feeling as being genuine without any references to poop or genitals. And I let him have his long paragraphs, with a few exceptions for the sake of dialogue. Mirbeau was a journalist, but our modern semiautomatic rules of journalistic style weren't fixed yet, perhaps because page design, much less web page design, hadn't been fixed yet either, and people didn't need to "break up long blocks of text" to compete with pop-up ads.

Deal with it. If your wee head needs a breather, go get a beer. (You may need a good deal of beer after you read this book; it's brilliant, but it's a killer.) You can leave a trail of breadcrumbs to the place where you left off if you really need to.

I even let Mirbeau keep his stacked narratives.

Switching topics to keep your attention for the moment, and dropping the crotchety-old-man sarcasm gradually as I do so, let the translator for a moment awkwardy assume the mantle of literary critic. An abused term, these days denoting either a gushing blurb writer or a deconstructionist out to destroy a canon; no, I just want to tell you a couple of things that might help you enjoy a text with which I have become almost uncomfortably intimate.

I've said Mirbeau was a journalist. Back then journalism and fiction weren't quite such divergent paths as they seem to have become now, for all but a few trust-fund-deficient and talented, and chronically impecunious—god damn it, I was going to mention the novelist-journalist Neal Pollack, and his recent absolutely brilliant humorous novel *Jewball*, and then the sentence was rammed into a comedic brick wall by fact that the Jewish money jokes are played out even when you crank them into reverse.

Baaaaah, screw the present and all of its denizens except *bien sûr* you, dear reader of the pre-existentialists (because if anyone would lay claim to that title, he must fight his way around Mirbeau). Let us concentrate on that stacked narrative.

The strangest thing about this book is that the framing narrative—the story that's wrapped around the main action—parallels said main action in plot, but disagrees with it logically on several key points. And since nearly every character in the book accuses nearly every other of being insane at least once, you would assume that every narrator within is more or less assumed to be unreliable by the ensemble cast itself. But since so much of the text is so closely related to Mirbeau's journalistic and autobiographical writing, is any of it essentially unreliable?

Augh!

But I fear these mysteries of process may be leading me further from the theme, while I ... *augh* again! No! These incongruencies *are* the theme! They fit perfectly!

The theme is the inability of art to grasp life, or of life to encompass art, or the disturbing things that art does when it pretends to speak from the ego when its roots are forever hidden in a fever-dream realm that's just outside the conscious mind. As modern writer Thomas Ligotti attempts to explain in his discussions of the uncanny, listening to a human consciousess trying to convince itself that it is real begins and ends as an attempt to focus on the hallucinations in one's peripheral vision.

The failure of the framed tale to jive logically with the main story . . . would the man who wrote *Diary of a Chambermaid* have done such a thing at random? No, the bizarre structure is no absinthe-and-paint-eating accident; the mismatch fits perfectly into the fetid futility of its heroes' beautiful but impossible attempts to escape from being the creatures they are. As the second-person hero of the interior frame says: You can't snub life, because life will have its revenge.

I tried to keep the footnotes to a dull roar, and in fact managed to pare them down to one explanation of a character's sarcastic reference to a contemporary artistic fad. This lone footnote was roughly 85% plagiarized from Pierre Michel of Angers, the greatest Mirbeau scholar my little existence will ever encounter, and the mastermind behind this translation project for lo these many years it's taken us to finally bring this lost masterwork into the multilingual global economy at last.

Mazel tov all around:

The aesthetic presentation of this book would have been gravely hampered were it not for the proofreading skills of Anita Dalton and the cover design by Kevin I. Slaughter. Thank you. Thanks also to Bob Helms for introducing me to the project fifteen or so years ago, to Claire Nettleton and Bob Ziegler for helping dig my original translation out of an untimely grave somewhere in New Zealand. (How the hell my manuscript got from Philadelphia where Helms lived to new Zealand is a mystery, but I had to redo most of it anyway; I was a stupid kid.) And double thanks to Pierre Michel; as far as I recall this whole thing was his idea, although it may have been Helms. I don't know, I just do the detail work.

Ann Sterzinger
May, 2015

ANN STERZINGER is an American novelist whose works include *NVSQVAM (nowhere)* and *The Talkative Corpse*. As an editor, she has worked with publications as wildly diverse as *The Chicago Reader, Temp Slave!,* and *Taki's Magazine*. She currently co-edits the Web-based journal *Trigger Warning*. Her science fiction novel *LYFE* will be released eventually.

CLAIRE NETTLETON, Ph.D., is a Visiting Assistant Professor in French Studies at Scripps College, specializing in the relationship between radical aesthetics and the Industrial Revolution. Her articles, on topics varying from Octave Mirbeau's automobile fiction to J.-K. Huysmans' environmental poetry, have appeared in *Nineteenth Century French Studies, Cahiers Octave Mirbeau,* and *Dix-Neuf.*

ROBERT ZIEGLER is professor emeritus of liberal studies with Montana Tech of the University of Montana. His is the author of two books on Octave Mirbeau: *The Nothing Machine: The Fiction of Octave Mirbeau,* and *Octave Mirbeau's Fictions of the Transcendental.*

OCTAVE MIRBEAU (1848–1917) was a prolific French novelist, playwright, and essayist. Known as an outspoken champion of unpopular causes, he embraced anarchism (authoring the anti-electoral pamphlet, *La Grève des électeurs*) and was an ardent defender of Alfred Dreyfus. As an art critic Mirbeau flouted received opinion, presciently recognizing the importance of such Impressionist and Post-Impressionist painters as Claude Monet, Paul Cézanne, and Vincent van Gogh (whose life and work loosely inspired *In the Sky*). Today Octave Mirbeau is best known as the author of the perennially controversial modern novels *Diary of a Chambermaid* and *The Torture Garden*, which was once described as "the most sickening work of art of the nineteenth century."

NineBandedBooks.com

L'ÉCHO DE PARIS

16e ANNÉE — N° 271

Mardi 2 Mai 1899

VALENTIN SIMOND
DIRECTEUR

JOURNAL LITTÉRAIRE ET POLITIQUE DU MATIN

RÉDACTION ET ADMINISTRATION : 16, RUE DU CROISSANT

Paris et Départements : 10 cent. le Numéro — Étranger : 15 cent.

ANNONCES, RÉCLAMES et FAITS DIVERS

Les manuscrits non insérés ne sont pas rendus

VALENTIN SIMOND
DIRECTEUR

ABONNEMENTS

Un mois ... 4 fr. | Trois mois ... 10 fr.

Adresser tout ce qui concerne la Rédaction au bureau de « L'ÉCHO DE PARIS », 16, rue du Croissant

Publicité de première et deuxième page exclusivement au bureau du journal

SOMMAIRE

DEMAIN MATIN

DANS LE CIEL

XXVII

CHRONIQUE

NOUVELLE A LA MAIN

30353045R00116

Printed in Great Britain
by Amazon